I0596476

The Promise of Us

The Promise of Us

W Mason Dunn

ISBN 979-8-9926856-3-3

"Trust in the LORD with all thine heart; and lean not unto thine own understanding."

Proverbs 3:5 (KJV)

Acknowledgments

First, I give all glory to my Heavenly Father. Thank You for the gift of writing, for trusting me with words that touch hearts, and for the platform and readers who make this journey possible. Every page is an offering back to You. Be glorified.

To my husband, Donald, and my children, Ashley and Michael— thank you for your love, patience, and steady support. You remind me that home is the truest kind of love story.

To Danyelle Scroggins, thank you for your wisdom and encouragement. Your words came at just the right time and carried me through the hard parts of the process.

Margo Thomas, thank you for your continued support and for reading my stories before the rest of the world sees them. Your honest feedback and enthusiasm mean more than you know.

And to Barbara Joe Williams, thank you for your wisdom and encouragement while editing. Your keen eye and kind spirit help shape these words into something beautiful.

To every reader who picked up *The Promise of Us*, thank you for letting these characters find a home in your heart. My prayer is that you feel hope on every page and remember that love, real love, is always worth the promise.

Table of Contents

Chapter 1

Laughter swirled around the room, welcoming and easy, but it snagged against the woman in the white jumpsuit and pumps.

"Open this one next," Dee said, thrusting a glittery bag into Lorraine's hands, her grin wide.

Lorraine's smile lit a beat too late. *Keep smiling. Don't let them see.* She pulled at the paper, layer by layer, until black satin trickled into her lap. A wave of squeals broke out. She elevated it skeptically, suspending the scandalous slip of fabric by its hanger.

"Is that a shawl?" her mother asked, voice caring, curious.

The response was a chorus of howls. Dee bent low, muttering with a playful glint in her eye. "No, ma'am, it's not. Lorraine's going to explain this to you afterward."

Helen pressed her hand to her cheek. If her complexion hadn't been so deep, it might have deceived her. "Oh, my. Maybe I should go tidy up the kitchen." She crept out, sparking another burst of giggles.

Lorraine thrust the garment back into its bag, her fingers fretting with the tissue. *Breathe. Smile. Pretend you're having fun.* Her eyes roamed the room. Balloons fastened in bouquets, pearl garlands capturing sunlight on the drapes, gifts piled across the coffee table filled the room with celebration. Yet, her chest felt tense, as though bound by a ribbon.

She opened each box the same way: *smile, nod, and a quick, "thank you."* But her laugh trailed a second too late, fingers tore tissue into slivers, and her gaze fixed on things that didn't matter. Dee noticed. Helen, too. *They can tell. They always can.*

"Open this one next." Another box slipped into her lap. Lorraine took a slow sip of punch, the sweetness sharp on her tongue, before stripping back the tissue. Red satin glittered up at her. Gasps and playful oohs filled the air as she raised the teddy.

I should be happy.

She delicately folded the teddy, tucking it back as though it might break, while her mind swirled, refusing to rest.

Four weeks.

One job offer.

Zero certainties.

And no peace in sight.

Chapter 2

3 days earlier

"I love my mom, but I know good and well she's about to hold me hostage in this house. I need an escape plan." Running on fumes, Lorraine pulled her car into her parents' driveway, tired and emotionally drained. Skipping a check-in was not an option.

A symphony of spicy tomatoes, sauteed onions, and sharp garlic met her at the door. *Stay strong. It's part of Mom's ploy to keep me here.*

Lorraine walked through the entryway into the living room. The leather sofa and loveseat were locked in place like natural landmarks. Her eyes fell upon childhood photos of her brother, Nathan, and herself, which were still displayed on the wall. The only difference was that they now included adorable pictures of Nathan's daughter, Clarissa. Everyone in the family loved and pampered the only grandchild.

Lorraine found her parents sitting at the dining room table reviewing documents. She dropped her keys into her purse as if she were walking into an ambush. Without saying a word, she glanced at the pot simmering on the stove. James and Helen Davis meant well. But from Lorraine's perspective, it felt very controlling.

"Hey, baby girl." Her father flashed a warm, welcoming smile. "We're just looking over the seating arrangement for the wedding."

"Hi, Lorraine," said her mother, pushing back from the table. "Have you eaten. I cooked spaghetti. I'll make you a plate."

I knew it!

"Mm-hmm. No, thank you. I stopped by a drive-thru for a burger and fries on my drive home," said Lorraine. *I won't let her keep me here longer than necessary.*

"Why don't you have a seat and tell us about your audit while you look over what we've done so far?" said Helen.

Another trick of the trade, getting me to talk about my work. But it wouldn't hurt to look over the seating chart.

Eyebrows lifting, Lorraine slipped into a seat at the table. "I'll sit, but I only have a few minutes. Just wanted to check on you guys. The audit went well, even though it took a long time. This client was a little shaky. They're either nervous about the process or hiding something. I'll know more when I complete the analysis. This project will look good in my employment file."

"Your hard work will pay off. I'm proud of you." A proud grin swept across her father's face.

Not too long ago, those words would have meant everything to me. But now I'm driven by my own desire to be the best. And that includes a position on the management team.

Scanning the seating chart, she mulled over every name. "I still don't understand why we invited Uncle Joe. And who is his plus one?"

Helen waved a hand in dismissal. "We don't need to know who he's bringing. Just give her a place to sit."

"Don't you remember what happened last time he brought a plus one to the family reunion?" asked Lorraine. "The woman tripped, knocked over Cousin Emma Jean, and they both rolled onto the floor."

"He's your grandfather's brother. Just send the invitation," said James, his attention focused on the document.

Uncle Joe didn't even show up for Grandpa's funeral. She dared not say it out loud.

"Certain folks are just awkward. Let's get through this list. Don't complicate matters," said Helen, frustration in her tone.

In four weeks and three days, Lorraine would marry Liam Whittington. She had fallen in love with the handsome, well-to-do landscaping business owner more than a year earlier. She wanted a storybook wedding. The price of her dream was more than enough family involvement. She was excited, but more than a little overwhelmed.

James and Helen were wonderful parents, offering their children boundless love and guidance. Everything was great until Lorraine got pregnant in high school. With persuasion from her parents, she gave the baby up for adoption after the birth. That's when the dynamics of their relationship changed for the worse. Her pregnancy and later adoption became the family's well-kept secret. It was also the start of Lorraine's realization that her voice didn't seem to matter, and her presence barely registered.

"I know we need to get this done," said Lorraine, releasing an irrepressible yawn. "But the audit took longer than expected. I'm tired and I want to go home."

Helen gave her daughter a pensive look. "Your father and I cleared our schedules so we could be available to help you with this. Be considerate."

I should've known she would dismiss my feelings.

"Don't you see? I'm exhausted and overwhelmed." The words flowed before she could hold them back.

"You're making everything harder than it needs to be. You're a little sensitive right now," said Helen, shaking her head.

Pointing a shaky finger to her chest, Lorraine said, "I'm sensitive because there's so much left to do for the wedding. And every time I come to you, you treat me like I'm being dramatic. But I'm drowning here. I'll see you guys later."

Lorraine stood, gathered her things, and walked out the door.

I hate feeling invisible. And I don't want to spend the rest of my life wondering if I matter. Besides, I love my parents; I do. But they don't know me. Not the way they think they do.

But Liam … he sees me. All of me. And he loves me anyway.

I want to be enough for him.

Chapter 3

Down the street and around the corner, Liam stood near the grill in his mother's backyard. Arms folded tight across his chest, the weight on his shoulder never quite settled. His brother, Donnie, flipped a T-bone steak with calm hands, laughter spilling freely as bright yellow, orange, and red flames flickered. Bubble juices rose around the edges of the meat, echoing small pops in the air.

For Liam, relaxation was like trying to smooth out a lawn that never stopped germinating weeds. The moment he pulled one thought, another sprouted in its place. Operating the family's landscaping business occupied most of his brainpower. When he wasn't contemplating logistics or creating job bids, he was managing operational tasks.

That was until he fell in love with Lorraine Davis, then his once drab life converted to Technicolor. She was his good thing the Scriptures referred to in Proverbs 18:22. Just being around her made his flesh burn with a passion he found difficult to contain. And in just a few more weeks, she would be his wife.

Donnie closed the grill cover and slid onto one of the red cushioned patio chairs.

"I hope you know what you're doing," said Liam, sitting in a chair across from his brother.

"Do I sense a hint of doubt?"

"No doubt, little brother." Liam looked out into the distance as if searching for something. "How long are you planning on staying in town?"

"I thought you would head to Hollywood after graduating from Florida Agricultural and Mechanical University."

"It's only been a few months. Besides, I wanted to wait until after the wedding."

"I appreciate that. But you know I don't want you to put your career on hold."

"Truth is, there are a lot of changes happening around here. You're getting married and moving out of Mom's house. Mom's dating Zeke. I want to make sure everyone gets settled before I leave."

"I'll keep an eye on Mom. Don't worry about that. Besides, Zeke seems to be a good guy. I think he's good for Mom."

"It's nice to see her smiling and loving life again."

Liam leaned back, eyes tracing the deep purple and blue hues bruising the dusky sky. The string lights above him purred softly, illuminating the trimmed hedges and freshly cut grass. Somewhere beyond the fence, a lawnmower droned a steady, familiar hum. For a heartbeat, the years crumpled, and he could almost see his ten-year-old self.

"I remember pushing my toy mower in dad's shadow as he cut the grass. His shadow would stretch tall over the grass and follow right behind. I would try to step perfectly inside his footprints. Every so often, Dad would glance over his shoulder and tell me that one day I would catch him. I'd grin wide, puff out my chest, certain that I could.

Sometimes, he would stop halfway across the yard. I'd stop beside him as he'd point at the neat lines across the grass. He'd say things like, 'Makes the yard look sharp.'"

Donnie gazed into the distance as if recalling his own memories. "He taught us a lot of lessons."

"I wanted to be just like Dad. Studied his every move. After finishing my MBA, I looked forward to joining him in the business. Never thought I'd be running it without him."

Donnie stared into his brother's eyes, revealing the sadness that lingered between them. "And you're doing a fine job, big brother. Dad would be proud."

"We spent a lot of time back here as kids building forts, playing army, and pretending the trampoline was a spaceship." Liam scanned the enclosed backyard as if each blade of grass held a priceless memory.

"Football and baseball …," said Donnie, shaking his head and smiling.

"And lots of cookouts with you and Dad at the grill." Liam smiled and crossed one leg over the other.

"Yes, we did." Donnie's eyes grew moist, but no tears fell. "I lost my desire to grill for a while. Brought back too many memories. Last year was the first time I grilled anything since Dad died."

"Well, it's good to have you back. Just don't burn anything." Liam teased.

Donnie tossed a pensive glance. "Maybe I should make your steak extra, extra crispy."

Liam laughed, then suddenly became serious. "It's good to see Mom getting back to her old self. Isn't it?"

"Yes, it is. She and Zeke spend almost as much time together as you and Lorraine."

Liam caught a whiff of the steaks, and his mouth watered. "Now we just have to find someone for you."

Donnie waved a finger in the air. "Don't worry about me. I have plenty of female companionship. If you know what I mean."

Shouting and laughter burst from the other side of the fence.

Liam turned his head toward the neighbor's yard and cupped his ear. "Do you hear that?"

"What?"

"The kids next door are playing outside."

Donnie nodded his head. "Yeah. The Wilsons' grandkids are visiting them again."

"I want that one day."

"Grandkids?"

"Sure, one day. But I was talking about a family." Liam clasped his hands together. "I want laughter in my backyard and kids running around everywhere. I want to create memories like the ones we had. And not just the good stuff. I want it all."

Donnie threw his head back and laughed. "Not me. I'm in no hurry to buckle down."

"I just keep thinking about Dad and Mom. They chose us, and it changed the trajectory of our lives," said Liam, releasing a wistful sigh.

For years, Harold and Daisy Whittington tried to conceive a child of their own. After several more years of being on the adoption waiting list, the agency informed them that a pair of brothers was looking for a home. The grateful adoptive parents made a vow to love and provide for their sons to the best of their abilities.

"That's true. But they were ready for the responsibility. I don't know if I ever will be."

"It's my purpose. God didn't rescue me to walk this life alone. I want a life where Lorraine and I build something together, kids and all." A slow, expectant smile swept across Liam's face as the possibilities unfolded in his mind.

"You'll make a brilliant father," said Donnie.

"That's the goal. I don't want to be the father our sperm donor turned out to be." His eyebrows furrowed.

"Neither do I," said Donnie, pointing to his chest. "That's why I'm going to wait. Don't want to be anything like him."

"Funny how two men can be so different from one another. One man fathers two boys and abandons them, while the other rescues them and loves them unconditionally. God turned it around for our good. I want to have a house full of children and love them the way Dad loved us. And even more importantly, the way God loves us."

***

Lorraine finally made it to her condominium. She kicked off her shoes and fell onto the couch.

"You look like you had a rough day." Dee dropped onto the loveseat and uncapped a bottle of water.

"It started with the audit. The client submitted boxes full of receipts and no financial statements."

Dee took a sip. "You would think they weren't expecting you."

"Which wasn't the case because someone scheduled the audit last week. We all wasted so much time."

"Well, you're home now." Dee offered an encouraging smile.

"Yes, I am. But I stopped by to see my parents first."

"How are they?"

"They're well. I was going to do a quick check-in and head home, but as always, Mom had other plans. She tried to keep me there for a while."

Dee grinned and leaned her head in Lorraine's direction.

"Be grateful. I wish my parents would spend more time with me."

A tinge of guilt made its way to Lorraine's heart. When Dee accepted Christ as her Savior, her mother declared she didn't need any holy roller trying to tell them how to live. Since then, their visits were few and far between. But that didn't stop Dee from praying for a reconciliation.

"Oh, Dee. I'm sorry. You're right. I should stop complaining about them."

"No worries. I don't want you to forget how blessed you are."

Lorraine glanced at her ringing phone. A smile appeared instantly on her face.

"Must be Liam," said Dee. "Because you look like a doting schoolgirl."

"Whatever." Lorraine scooped up her shoes and skipped toward her bedroom.

Dee chuckled and cocked her head in Lorraine's direction. "I thought you were exhausted. Where did the sudden burst of energy come from?"

Lorraine stuck out a mimicking tongue at Dee, then answered the call.

"Hey, baby," her voice sang.

"Just checking in with my bride."

"I just got in a few minutes ago. Went by to see Dad and Mom." Lorraine tossed her shoes in the closet. Lodging the phone between her shoulder and chin, she checked her appearance in the dresser mirror.

"How are they?"

"Great," said Lorraine, swallowing her complaints. "Did you get to see your mother?"

"Only for a moment. She was leaving with Zeke. So, Donnie and I threw a couple of steaks on the grill."

"Nice." She fell onto the corner chair, crisscrossing her legs.

"I know you're just getting in, so I'll give you time to relax. But I wanted to know if you would have dinner with me tomorrow night?"

"Let me check my calendar," she teased. "Of course I will. What should I wear?"

"Something casual. But bring a jacket. We'll be dining outdoors."

"Only in Tallahassee can one dine outside in the middle of December and still be comfortable," said Lorraine with a playful giggle. "Where are we going?"

"It's a surprise."

He's so romantic. Constantly leaving handwritten notes, sending sweet, unexpected texts, and arranging surprise dinner plans.

"Just promise me you'll always be this romantic," she said just above a whisper.

"I won't just promise. I'll practice every day. It won't always be fancy. But it will be real.

Lorraine closed her eyes, letting his voice soothe her. Yet somewhere beneath the sweetness, fear whispered that love doesn't always last.

Chapter 4

The Thursday morning traffic flowed easily. Streetlights blinked green without argument, and even the city seemed to exhale. The usual tension of the commute had thinned. If the traffic was any sign, almost the entire city was on winter break.

With hands fixed on the steering wheel, Lorraine felt the customary writhe in her chest. Part remorse, part resolve. Her mind turned over the words she wished she could rewind and speak correctly. The city blurred past in streaks of sunlight and shadow as she inhaled, letting it settle in her chest before exhaling. Finally, she pressed the button on the dashboard. The soft hum of OnStar filled the car. She mumbled, "Call Mom."

"Hello?"

"Hi, Mom."

"How are you, dear?"

"I'm fine." Lorraine smiled as she drove past Starbucks. Liam and she spent a lot of time there at the beginning of their relationship. The memories warmed her heart.

"I apologize for my nasty mood last night. I was tired, but that's no excuse for my behavior."

"Thanks for saying that. But I get it. Planning a wedding can be exhausting. Is there anything I can do to help?"

I appreciate the offer, Mom. But you go overboard with your help.

"There's nothing you can do. The coordinator is handling everything. Besides, you're letting us have the bridal shower at the house. I really appreciate that. My place is too small."

"No problem. I'm happy to do it."

"What do you have planned for today?"

Lorraine drove around a slow-moving vehicle and pulled onto Capital Circle.

"I have Bible Study this morning. If the weather holds up, your father and I will take a walk this afternoon."

"Well, have fun. I need to get off the phone. Almost at work."

"Okay. I'll talk to you later."

"Love you, Mom."

"Love you, too."

She drove the rest of the way thinking of the many things left to do before the wedding.

We need to get the license, get a final head count, do a walk-through, and I must break in my wedding shoes.

In four weeks, it'll all be over, and I'll be Mrs. Lorraine Davis Whittington. Wonder what that will be like. I've been single for so long. I've been making my own decisions and doing what I want, when I want, for so long, I wonder what it will be like to include Liam in all of that? Thank God for premarital counseling. At least we know what to expect.

Lorraine eased into the Hamilton and Dunn parking lot, her first and only job after graduating from college. She dispersed a series of good mornings to colleagues before settling into her cubicle. Stacks of after-action reports, unreconciled financial reports, and unread new tax regulations vied for her attention. When she finally took a break, it was lunchtime. Dee stood at her cubicle, whining like a hungry puppy.

"What's for lunch?" asked Dee.

"I'm skipping lunch today. I had to spend the morning double-checking my client's records since they didn't have all their information gathered when I arrived. Now I need to review the audit findings for my meeting with Mr. Holloway."

"When's the meeting?" asked Dee, her voice whiny with displeasure.

"In the morning. You know what?"

"What's that?"

"When I become a senior auditor," said Lorraine, shaking a finger in the air. "I'll notify clients of the extra fees for their unprepared documents. When the clients don't prepare, they cause us extra work."

"I hear you, Roomie. I didn't realize you were still interested in the senior auditor position."

"I am and I'm not."

"Okay," said Dee, dragging out the syllables with sarcasm in her voice.

"I still think they robbed me of the position last year when they gave it to Kawana. We scored the same on the exam."

"Maybe next time."

"There won't be another senior auditor position available for a while. Besides, Liam and I've been talking about starting a family right away."

"That's sweet. The two of you will make beautiful children. I'm headed to Subway. Would you like me to bring you something back?"

"That would be great. I'll take a veggie salad. Liam's planning a special dinner, and I don't want to ruin my appetite."

"You two are totally disgusting. And I hope God has another one just like Liam looking for me."

"I'm sure God already has a husband in mind for you. Just be patient."

"I know you're right. Besides, I don't want him unless God sends him." Dee strapped her Coach purse over her shoulder. "I'll be right back with your salad."

"Thanks." Lorraine watched her friend leave, returning to the mountain of work waiting for her.

When Dee returned, Lorraine was nearly done.

"I asked for ranch and Italian dressing. Wasn't sure which one you wanted." Dee placed Lorraine's lunch on the desk.

"Thanks. How much do I owe you?" asked Lorraine, reaching for her purse.

"You can buy my lunch next time." Dee took a couple of steps out of the cubicle. "Don't forget about the team meeting this afternoon."

"Thanks for the reminder," said Lorraine, glancing at her watch. "Three o'clock, right?"

"Right."

"I think I'll head home after that so I can get a jump on getting ready. I want to be dressed when Liam stops by to pick me up for dinner."

***

A little after six o'clock, Liam tapped on Lorraine's door.

Tugging at his lightweight charcoal turtleneck sweater, he thought, *Maybe I should have worn the blue sweater. She likes that one. It's too late to change my mind now. When she sees what I have planned for the evening, the color of my sweater will be the last thing on her mind.*

Lorraine opened the door with a warm smile that sent a quiver down his spine. She wore a cream sweater and brown pants that hugged her in all the right places. Loose curls fell from the messy bun on the top of her head. He fought the overwhelming urge to plant butterfly kisses on her bare neck.

"You look amazing," said Liam, his heartbeat doubling.

"Thank you."

In a moment of pure desire, he leaned in, devouring her lips with a passionate kiss. "I can't wait to come home to you every night."

"I'm looking forward to that, too."

Controlling his thoughts, Liam took a deep breath and changed the subject. "Let's go, sweetheart. I hope you're hungry."

"Where are we going?"

"You'll know in about fifteen minutes." He locked the door before leading her down the stairs and to his SUV, sneaking in one more kiss before she slid into the passenger side.

Liam walked around to the driver's side and slid behind the steering wheel.

Lorraine wrinkled her forehead. "There are quite a few places we can drive to in fifteen minutes."

"Patience, my love." He started the engine and reached for her hand. She smiled, and it was fuel for his soul. Lorraine had broken down every wall he'd placed around his heart.

Liam watched as her face filled with amazement the moment he pulled into a Lake Ella parking spot.

"I never would have guessed you were bringing me here."

"We've only just begun, my love." Liam exited the car and headed to the other side.

The December air held an unexpected warmth as they strolled the path beside Lake Ella. The hush of the evening wrapped around them. Holiday lights twinkled like stars around the nearby cottages, each built in 1925 and renovated into a charming shop or restaurant. Leon's at Lake Ella loomed ahead, glowing with golden light. Closed to the world, the restaurant was entirely theirs for the evening.

Liam opened the restaurant door, allowing her to enter. He grinned as her puzzled eyes searched the empty restaurant. His eyes scanned the rustic charm of tables flickering with votive lights. A hint of cinnamon and pine clung gently to the air. In the corner stood a tall Christmas tree decorated with gold and ivory ornaments.

"Wow," she murmured. "This is beautiful."

The smooth, sultry sound of the jazz floated from around the corner. Lorraine's eyes widened, and she turned toward him. He smiled and took her hand.

"Where is everyone?" she asked.

Before Liam could answer, a welcoming voice rang out, "Good evening. I'm George." A tall man with a kindhearted nod greeted them. "We've been expecting you."

George led them through the empty restaurant, through a pair of doors that opened onto a private deck—outside, the lake shimmered under the evening light. A table awaited, draped in linen and surrounded by candles. Two empty champagne glasses sparkled in the candlelight. The soft crackling of a fire pit sat a few feet away.

Liam approached the table and pulled a chair out for Lorraine.

"Where is everyone?" She asked again, sliding into the seat.

"It's just us. I reserved the entire restaurant for us," said Liam, moving to his own chair.

"Liam …" she whispered his name. "Thank you so much. This is amazing."

He leaned forward, reaching for her hand. "This is only the beginning. I love you. I plan to spend the rest of my life making you happy."

***

Words escaped Lorraine. The music, the glow of the fire pit, the lake in front of her, and the man across the table from her were the perfect setting for a romantic evening. Her eyes lingered on the water, not really looking at anything. Her mind drifted to all the ways Liam made the night feel like a promise. The music wrapped around her, and she could feel the gentleness of his hand stroking hers.

"Good evening, Mr. Whittington, Miss Davis."

Lorraine flinched before turning to see the gentleman at the front door. "Oh! You caught me in a moment. This place is beautiful," she said.

"No problem. My name is Marcus. I'll be your server for the evening. We have chilled champagne to toast the season. If you need anything at all, I'll be nearby. Mr. Whittington has carefully planned everything you see. The evening is all yours." He offered a warm smile before stepping away.

Liam raised the champagne bottle and filled Lorraine's glass before his own. His eyes locked on hers. "To the promise of us."

She clinked her glass against his. "To the promise of us."

After taking a sip, Lorraine sat silent for a moment. Taking it all in.

"What are you thinking?" asked Liam.

"Do you ever wonder why God brought us together? We could have lived our entire lives without ever meeting each other. However, I was assigned to audit your financial records."

Liam reached over and squeezed her hand. "I believe it was a divine set-up. There are no coincidences. I'd been asking God to help me find a wife. And I believe you are the answer to my prayer."

"Well, I wasn't looking for or thinking about a relationship."

"But you just couldn't resist me, could you?" Liam chuckled.

Shaking her head, Lorraine took a sip. "You're kidding. But I really couldn't. I tried to fight it. But I couldn't get you out of my head. And now you're a permanent resident in my heart."

"Let's agree to always seek God first. He knows what's best for us."

"I agree." Lorraine nodded. "And I'm so glad we chose a Christian pre-marital counselor. She's taught me so much about what to expect once we're married."

Liam looked up as the server approached the table. The server carried two bowls. They were deep, filled with golden She Crab soup. The server placed Lorraine's bowl down first, nodding politely, then he set Liam's in front of him. Delicate swirls of steam rose from each of the bowls. "I'll give you a few minutes to enjoy," said Marcus.

"Thank you," said Liam.

They joined hands, and he blessed the food.

Lorraine raised her spoon and took a sip when she noticed Liam staring at her.

"Do I have something on my face?"

"No. I was thinking, I hope our daughters have your eyes."

"Daughters? What about a son? How many children do you want?" she asked.

"One of each for starters?"

"For starters?" Lorraine frowned.

"Let's just say, I want as many as we can afford. And I want them as soon as we get married. How about you?"

"The timing is great. I want to start a family right away. I'll take a leave of absence from work during the children's formative years. But we'll need to talk about the number of children."

A flicker of a memory rushed in, uninvited—the baby girl she gave up for adoption.

Liam leaned forward, his voice low. "You're thinking about her, aren't you?"

His words brought her to the present. She felt no shame. Just an honest ache for a child she loved. "Yes."

"She was your first," he said.

Lorraine swallowed. Overcome by the reality of being seen and loved for who she was, a gentle twinge rose in her throat.

Tears filled her eyes. "You're the only one who really sees me for who I am. You get me."

Lorraine's heart sank. He loved her. And she loved him and would do anything to make him happy.

Marcus returned. "Here we are. Handmade fettuccine tossed with olive oil and herbs, topped with mojo-styled roasted chicken, and shaved parmesan. A warm meal for a beautiful night."

Laughter, light banter, and dreams of their future together filled the rest of their meal. When they stepped out of the restaurant after dinner, the evening wrapped around them like an embrace as they strolled to the car.

The night air carried the hope of their future. And this was only the beginning.

Chapter 5

Friday morning, employees rushed to their duty stations. Clients filled the waiting area. An impatient deliveryman tapped the elevator button. Members of the cleaning service wiped down high-touch surfaces.

Lorraine stepped toward the reception desk, offering a smile before speaking. "Good morning, Patricia."

"Hey, Lorraine. I see you coming up in here dancing and smiling like you in a Disney movie. Must be nice."

"I had a great evening. How about you?"

"I did, too." Patricia shook her head and pulled a document from the printer stand. "Getting ready to go on vacation next week."

"Can't wait to hear all about it. I'll let you get to work," said Lorraine, reaching for a wrapped mint from the counter. "Talk to you later." She pivoted toward the elevator, making eye contact with the delivery guy.

"Good morning, and thank you for holding the door."

He nodded, gave a disgruntled grunt, sucking the air from the cage. Lorraine wasn't sure if he was having a tough morning or if his personality was uncouth. Either way, she was determined to enjoy the rest of her morning. When the doors flew open, she went one way, and he went the other.

She made her way down the hall and into the large maze of staff auditor's cubicles. The room buzzed with the hum of conversations, ringing phones, and the rhythmic tapping of keyboards. Lorraine's desk, like many others, displayed small reminders of life beyond work. A framed photo of Liam and her at her parents' anniversary party sat on the corner of her desk, and a Grambling State University mug sat next to it. Her eyes drifted toward the offices lining the walls. *I'll make it there one day.*

She asked to be added to the list the last time a senior auditor's position became available. Lorraine spent most of her free time studying for the exam. She aced the exam, but so did Kawana. After all the hard work and dedicated time, Hamilton and Dunn gave the position to her colleague. They promised to consider her for the next senior auditor opening without having to take the exam. But that was over a year ago.

Now that she was planning a future with Liam that included growing a family, she decided the position did not offer the work/life balance she longed for. But now and then, she couldn't help but think about how she was more qualified than Kawana.

After greeting a few colleagues, she settled in and powered up the computer. She glanced around her cubicle, the narrow walls shutting her in like a fortress. The L-shaped desk was genuinely tidy. A small cabinet loomed overhead. Its drab gray doors added nothing to the modest setting. Her eyes wandered to the hard plastic visitor chair wedged beside the desk. Its unforgiving legs wobbled a bit if anyone shifted their weight.

Staff auditors interpreted accounting records for the financial statements. When they weren't interpreting accounting records, they dealt with tax and regulatory changes. It was all these things that she loved about her job. Lorraine logged on to her computer and worked for the next two hours, filing reports for her current assignment.

"What's going on, Roomie?"

Lorraine looked up to find Dee smiling back at her.

"Hey."

"I guess I won't be calling you Roomie much longer." Dee flopped into the visitor's chair.

"Nope, but you can always call me a friend."

Dee shook her head in agreement. "That's right. And don't you forget it."

"You should move into my room when I leave. That way, your new housemate can have the smaller room." Lorraine waved a finger in the air.

"Already planning on it. How much will my rent increase with the larger room?"

"I'm not increasing your rent."

"What are you talking about. It makes good business sense." Dee's voice was stern as she leaned forward.

"You let me worry about that. I just need you to help me find a good housemate."

"You can count on me," said Dee, gazing at the stack of documents on Lorraine's desk. "What are you working on?"

"Going over my documentation so I can discuss the audit findings for my last assignment with Mr. Holloway."

"What time's the meeting?"

Lorraine glanced at the time on her monitor. "In ten minutes."

"Oh. Then I'll let you get back to work."

When it was time for the meeting, she took a deep breath and headed for Mr. Holloway's office. He was a unique individual. Although socially awkward, he was intelligent, kind, and well-meaning. It was his job to accept or reject her recommendation. She took a deep breath and knocked on the closed door.

"Come in."

Lorraine entered and closed the door, subduing the noise from the corridor of staff auditors.

I could accomplish a lot working in a quiet space like this.

Lorraine scanned the drab office. There were no plants, family photos, or anything to show Mr. Holloway had a life outside of Hamilton and Dunn.

He didn't bother to look away from his computer screen.

Lorraine eased into the chair and waited, ready to defend her assessment.

Steve Holloway sat firmly, looking in her direction. "I reviewed your report and agree with your findings," he said, offering a stiff smile. "You do good work."

Lorraine held back a satisfied grin. "Thank you, sir."

"Your efforts are commendable ..." He stopped mid-sentence as if to gather his thoughts. "One of our senior auditors has given notice. The position will be available after the first of the year. As I promised last year, after you, I mean after Kawana .... I told you I would consider you without requiring you to retake the exam. Are you still interested in the position?"

In that moment, Lorraine realized she hadn't given up hope of becoming a senior auditor.

She paused, unsure how to respond. She'd made promises to Liam without considering the possibility of the offer. Now she couldn't help but wonder if she would ever have this opportunity again.

"We promised you a shot at it without retaking the exam. If you aren't interested, Human Resources will post the position."

Loraine cleared her throat. "I understand." She paused and then asked, "May I have time to think about it?"

"You have two weeks."

She chuckled. "Two weeks!"

"Keep in mind, Lorraine. Last year, I convinced the Human Resources director to reconsider your application for the next opportunity. You're being offered the job as a favor to me."

"I understand," she said, her voice shaky.

"That's all I have. If you have nothing else for me, you can get back to work."

Lorraine rose from the chair. She steadied the documents with one hand against her chest. Reaching the door, she turned back toward Mr. Holloway and said, "Thank you."

He grunted and nodded in her direction.

Lorraine exited and closed the door behind her. Heart racing, she practically sprinted to her cubicle.

Am I dreaming, or did he just offer me the senior auditor's position? Who's leaving? Who cares? I'll have a nice salary increase and an office. I can't wait to tell Liam.

She reached for her phone and found a message from Liam. *"Work might have my time, but you will always have my heart. Just wanted to remind you of that."*

An anxious knot dropped to the pit of her stomach.

If I accept the offer, it'll shatter our dream of starting a family right away. I had hoped to be home with my children during their formative years. Looking forward to playtime, naptime, first steps, and first words. I want to do all the things I didn't get to do with the daughter I gave up for adoption. How can I do that if I'm busy working as a senior auditor?

I will spend my time supervising teams, presenting recommendations to upper management, and ensuring compliance with tax regulations. Instead of potty-training Junior, I'll be training staff auditors.

I need to talk to Liam.

She took a second look at his text before replying, *"Let's have lunch."*

Chapter 6

An hour later, Liam leaned back in his office chair. Lorraine seldom brought lunch to the office, but he enjoyed it when she did. He heard her voice ringing from the reception area. Lorraine usually stopped to chat for a few minutes with Sophia, the receptionist. After clearing a few things from the desk, he gravitated to the reception area.

How can she possibly be more beautiful every time I see her?

Their eyes met, sending goosebumps up and down his arms. She wore an elegant white satin blouse with a draped collar, exposing her long, beautiful neck. His gaze dropped to the black skirt hugging her body just enough to pique his imagination.

Lord, please, help me control my thoughts.

Lorraine reached for a large Chick-fil-A bag from the reception counter.

As if on cue, Liam rushed to retrieve the bag for her.

Liam led Lorraine down the hall into his office and closed the door. Dropping the bag on the desk, he drew her into his arms. He lowered his mouth until it hovered over hers. She parted her lips, sending an unspoken welcome. With a brief hesitation, he offered a passionate kiss. Before long, they were devouring each other's mouths. Then he remembered his prayer from minutes earlier.

"Just a few more weeks," he muttered, pulling away hesitantly.

They'd both vowed to follow God's plan and delay having sex until after the wedding. Some days were more difficult than others. This was one of the difficult times.

"Just a few more weeks," she whispered in agreement.

His flesh wanted to have its way. But he took a deep breath, pulled out the chair that sat in front of his desk for Lorraine to sit. Then he opened the office door wide before sitting himself opposite the desk.

Lorraine giggled shyly before retrieving their meals from the bag and placing them on the desk. "This doesn't compare to last night's feast, but I brought you two chicken sandwiches."

"It was a feast, wasn't it?"

"I can't stop thinking about it. Everything was perfect."

"You're the reason it felt perfect."

"You say the sweetest things, Mr. Whittington." Lorraine removed her salad from the bag and placed it on the desk in front of her.

After blessing the food, Liam took a large bite of one of his sandwiches. "I'm glad you suggested lunch. I don't know if I would've stopped working otherwise. Besides, I didn't think I would see you until tonight at your place. What game are we playing?"

"Dominos. Should be fun," she said, stirring in a dab of ranch dressing to her salad. "Have you been busy?"

"Yes, I have been. How about you? You been busy?"

"Pretty mundane. That is, until I met with Mr. Holloway."

"To review audit findings, right? How'd that go?"

"Mr. Whittington?" Sophia's voice called over the intercom.

Liam paused with his sandwich halfway to his mouth. He lowered it slowly. "I'm having lunch, Sophia."

"I understand; however, Mr. Wyatt wishes to meet you. He says it should only take a minute."

"Thank you. I'll be right there." He re-wrapped the sandwich and looked at Lorraine. "I'm sorry. He's one of our long-term customers. I should see what he wants."

"I understand. I'll be here." Lorraine released an impulsive smile as if grateful for the interruption.

Liam wiped his hand and mouth before pulling away from the desk. He walked out the door, waving an apologetic hand in the air.

***

Lorraine toyed with her salad. *I know he'll be happy for me. After all, he was there throughout the entire process last year. He helped me study for the exam. Liam comforted and encouraged me when I didn't get the job. He'll understand.*

Minutes later, Liam returned, pulling her out of her thoughts. He slipped behind his desk and tapped on the keyboard. "I need to make a note of this so I won't forget," he mumbled.

Lorraine took a few bites of her salad, contemplating how to deliver the news.

After a few clicks on the keyboard, Liam turned his full attention to Lorraine. "Sorry about that. You were telling me about the meeting with Mr. Holloway. Did he agree with your findings?"

"He did. No questions, concerns, or changes," she said with a hint of pride in her tone.

"That's great. You're a competent auditor, and he knows it."

Liam reached into the desk drawer, pulled out a tiny packet, and offered it to her. The packet crumpled when she touched it. It weighed little, and the contents inside shifted like tiny beads.

"What's this?" she asked.

"Look inside."

Lorraine tilted her head and opened the packet.

"I need your help," she said, staring curiously.

Liam chuckled. "Mustard seeds."

"Thank you, but …"

"If we have faith as a grain of mustard seed…" Liam began quoting Matthew 17:20.

Lorraine interjected, "… We shall say unto the mountain, remove hence to yonder place; and it shall remove."

"And nothing shall be impossible unto you." They completed the verse together.

"Imagine what we can accomplish when we put our faith together?" His eyes met hers and locked.

"I'd say we've accomplished a lot already," said Lorraine.

"I agree. That includes buying a house. I spoke to the realtor about the closing. Everything is going according to schedule."

Lorraine poked a few pieces of lettuce. "We're working on a tight schedule with the wedding and all."

"She knows we want to spend our first night as husband and wife in our new home," said Liam.

"How are we ever going to fill all those rooms?" An optimistic smile spread across Lorraine's face as the possibilities unfolded in her mind.

"A little at a time. Of course, we'll furnish the nursery right away."

They halted the discussion at the sound of Sophia's heels clanging down the hall.

"Just dropping off the mail." She placed a stack of documents on the corner of Liam's desk.

He turned his attention to the unopened envelope she'd faced down at the top of the stack. He retrieved the sealed envelope and turned it over. No return address. Written in the lower left-hand corner in big red letters were the words, PERSONAL AND CONFIDENTIAL.

"Thank you," he said, offering a questioning look.

"Wonder what this is about?" he muttered, showing the message to Lorraine.

"Personal and confidential," she said.

"The only admirer I want is you. I'll open it later. Besides, we're in the middle of a discussion."

Lorraine finished the salad, cleaned her mouth and hands, and then discarded the container. "I know you're curious about the letter. I can see it on your face. You should open it. Might be important."

Liam turned his attention to the envelope. Prying it open, he claimed the handwritten document.

Lorraine watched his inquisitive eyes fall to the bottom of the page, assuming he was eager to learn the sender's name. That's when his bottom lip almost dropped to the floor.

"What's the matter? Who's it from?" asked Lorraine.

"My biological father."

Liam's posture stiffened, and his shoulders squared like he was bracing for impact. He read the letter silently. Tension from their earlier conversation still lingered, but now something heavier settled between them. Whatever was in the letter had shaken him. His eyes scanned the page, fast at first, and then slowly.

His fingers gripped the letter tighter, crinkling the edges. She sensed a storm brewing.

He'll let me in when he's ready.

"Unbelievable!" Liam spat the words, hurling the letter to the desk like a nasty wad of slime.

Lorraine hurried around the desk and embraced him.

"You can read it," he said, pulling away and pointing to the document.

Hand trembling, Lorraine seized the discarded page.

Dear Liam,

It's been a while since we've seen each other, but I want to make up for lost time. Thought it would be better to contact you first since you're the oldest.

I thought it would be better to mail this letter to your office instead of your home since you don't live alone.

I'm glad to know that you're doing well running the business, and Donnie is doing well with his recent graduation. My boys are out here making me proud.

I know you're about to get married. Would love to meet my future daughter-in-law.

I'm staying at the Motel 6 on Apalachee Parkway—room 249. I would love it if you dropped by sometime soon.

Your real father,

Curtis Barnes

"Oh, babe. I don't know what to say."

"He had the audacity to sign it, your real father," said Liam, gesturing air quotes. "Harold Whittington was my real father. He did more for me than this sperm donor ever did. And if he thinks he's going to enter my life after all this time, he's wrong." Liam clenched his fist, opened it, then closed it.

"I know you're upset. Let's sit for a minute."

Liam returned to his seat. Lorraine reached across the desk, her hand found his in quiet comfort.

After a few moments, he squeezed her hand before letting go. "Thank you."

"What are you thinking?"

Liam stared into the distance. "This guy obviously has an agenda."

"I get that." She shook her head. "Do you think he reached out to Donnie?"

"Doesn't sound like it from the letter, but I'll have to ask Donnie. I just don't want my mother to get wind of this. She's been through enough. And she's finally found someone who makes her happy. If she finds out this Curtis guy is around, I don't know how she'll react."

"You can't control whether he reaches out to your mother."

Liam cocked an eyebrow. "If he knows what's good for him, he won't." Anger filled his every word.

"Do you plan to contact him?"

"Absolutely not!"

"You could tell him how you feel and find out what he really wants. I'm not telling you what to do. The decision is yours. I'm just asking you to consider meeting him. If anything, it could provide closure."

He faced her. "I don't need closure!"

Lorraine's heart sank. She loved him and would do anything to help. But for now, all she could do was give him time to process.

She frowned, and then, sensing his frustration, glanced at her watch. "I'll give you some time to process everything. I should probably return to my office."

"Thanks for understanding. I'll see you at your place tonight."

"Of course." She placed a tender kiss on his lips, gathered her belongings, and walked out the door.

Chapter 7

Curtis slumped down onto the flimsy mattress, causing the springs to creak under his weight. The ceiling fan above him was crooked and rotated; its steady click like a car turn signal left on too long. Freedom was supposed to feel better than this.

His thoughts carried him back to the courtroom many years ago.

Bam!

The judge pounded her gavel with authoritative force. "I hereby terminate the rights of the father."

"What's she talking about?" Curtis asked his court-appointed lawyer. The woman appeared young enough to be his daughter.

"Since you've failed to maintain contact or provide support, the court considers it abandonment," she said.

The judge's words freed me from an obligation I never really wanted. Everyone in the courtroom, including me, knew the judge's decision was best for the boys. First, their mother stole them from me. Then, that uppity Whittington couple stole them from me. Adopted them right from under me.

A couple arguing outside his window pulled him back into the motel room. Curtis sat up, rubbing the top of his head. He reached for a cigarette.

My boys are here in Tallahassee. We're breathing the same air.

He took a drag from the cigarette and then whispered, "I shoulda have never given up."

He sat on the edge of the bed, elbows on his knees, staring at the phone lying on the nightstand.

Liam runs his own business, and Donnie just graduated from college. They're men now, not boys. But they're still my sons.

Liam should have the letter by now. Even put my room number in it, and I still haven't heard from him.

Bet he won't call. That's their mother's fault; she probably talked trash about me.

Curtis rubbed a hand across his face. They smelt of cigarettes, ashes, and regret.

He paused at the dresser mirror. An older, leaner man stared back. He didn't see the father he remembered being. He saw a stranger who had failed every chance that mattered.

Maybe I'll write to Donnie. No, Liam will probably call before Donnie gets the letter. I'll give him a few more days to reach out to me, then I'll call.

I want the time back that was stolen from me.

The words hung heavy. Because now the question was whether he could finally get it.

Chapter 8

Sitting at the kitchen table in her condominium, Lorraine's heart beat with an erratic rhythm. Earlier, she and Dee hustled into the kitchen, preparing snacks and drinks for their monthly game night. Her thoughts flipped from Liam and the letter from his birth father to Mr. Holloway's promotion offer and back again. She tried to hide her worry, but Dee sensed that something was wrong.

"What's on your mind, roomie?" Dee's voice was marked with care.

"Oh, just the wedding," said Lorraine. "Time seems to fly by."

"It'll be fine. There are a lot of us working hard to make sure your day turns out perfect."

"Thanks." Lorraine pinned on a smile and placed a stack of napkins on the counter.

Before long, boxes of savory pizza, a tub of buttery popcorn, and dozens of baked cookies covered the kitchen counter. Playful banter mixed with the low hum of jazz music infiltrated the atmosphere.

Liam tossed the domino tiles on the table, setting the stage for another round of fun. Four eager sets of hands reached into the pile.

Lorraine sat next to Liam, exchanging flirty glances and gentle touches. Brandon sat on the other side of Lorraine. As a police officer, he preferred a clear view of the entrance. Even with his protective antennae working, he wore a competitive smirk aimed across the table at Liam. Dee, seated to Brandon's left and directly across from

Lorraine, leaned forward with a mischievous glint in her eye, positioning the double six in the center of the table.

"Remember, it's not about who wins or loses," said Lorraine.

Tonight was the last pre-wedding game night for the quartet. For over a year, the foursome met at Lorraine's condominium once a month. Sometimes, they played partners and sometimes they played singles. Tonight, it was men against women.

"That may be how you feel," said Dee. "But as your friend and domino partner, I need to let you know I'm in it to win it."

Lorraine and Dee had been college roommates, both majoring in accounting. After graduation, Hamilton and Dunn Financial Services in Tallahassee, Florida, hired both of them. Later, Lorraine purchased a condominium and invited Dee to move in with her. After her upcoming wedding, Lorraine would move out of the condo and into the home she and Liam were currently purchasing.

"You don't expect us to believe that, do you? There's no way you're going to win tonight," said Brandon, casting a mocking grin in Dee's direction and a domino tile on the table.

He and Lorraine grew up in the same neighborhood. They attended the same elementary, junior, and high schools. Later, Brandon joined the Tallahassee police force. They were both surprised to find out they lived in the same condominium.

When it was his turn, Liam eyed the tiles in his hand before placing one on the table. "You can't seriously expect to beat the dynamic duo. You can't beat the champs. Now give me fifteen!" He reached across the table, offering Brandon a high-five.

Lorraine retrieved the nearby pen and added their points to the score sheet. She'd volunteered to be scorekeeper, but as she recorded another fifteen points to their already leading record, she second-guessed her decision.

Dee held a domino above the table before playing it. "The next time we get together for game night, you two will be Mr. and Mrs. Whittington."

"And we'll be playing in your new home," added Brandon.

"You should probably call first," teased Liam, leaning toward Lorraine. "We might be otherwise engaged."

Lorraine blushed. She recognized that look in his eyes. It was that look that got him kicked out of the condo and on his way many nights. Their desire for one another was sweltering. But both vowed to wait until marriage. So, they'd been creative about spending time with one another and not placing themselves in a compromising position. It wasn't easy, but they believed it would be worth it.

It'd been a long time since Lorraine had felt such desire for a man. After being hurt and humiliated by her ex-boyfriend, Reggie, she shunned the thought of finding a decent man. Then one day, she received an assignment to conduct a financial audit for Whittington Landscaping. Liam was easy to look at with his smooth, dark-chocolate complexion and big brown eyes. His deep baritone voice gave her goosebumps. But she was there on assignment and forced herself to remain focused. Lorraine enjoyed her job as an auditor and was good at it. She dreamed of moving up the ladder. But after being passed over for a promotion, hopes and dreams of advancement waned.

"Did you make an offer on the house you guys were looking at?" asked Brandon.

"Yes." Liam ran a hand over his face when a move didn't go his way. "We made an offer on a four-bedroom off Bannerman Road."

"Four bedrooms? That's a lot of space," said Dee.

"We want children." Lorraine snapped her fingers, realizing she'd missed out on points.

"And lots of them," said Liam, spreading his arms wide.

Lorraine turned to Liam and shook her head. "That's a relative term. A lot to me, may not be a lot to you."

"I know. But I'm looking forward to being fruitful and multiplying. Which is why y'all need to call the house before coming over," said Liam, pointing from Brandon to Dee and then back again.

Liam turned to Lorraine. His eyes shone with a mix of excitement and apprehension, as if asking, "Are we really about to start this adventure together?"

Sensing his unspoken thought, she tossed a reassuring smile, her eyes saying, "Yes, and I wouldn't have it any other way."

"Enough with the googly eyes," said Dee. "I need you to stay focused, girlfriend. Are you going to stop them from winning?"

"I'm doing my best." Lorraine scanned her dominoes. "I can only play the hand I'm dealt."

Lorraine swallowed her thoughts, shook her head, and played her turn. Liam was everything she wanted in a husband. Smart, athletic, thoughtful, and most of all, he loved God.

She'd made poor choices in the past. Poor decisions led to an unexpected pregnancy during her senior year of high school. Out of love, Lorraine chose adoption so the baby could have a better life. God turned everything around, and the family moved forward. When Liam entered her life, it took some work to convince her parents that he was more than a fling. They quickly learned that he was not only good for her, but their love was pure and genuine. Now, everyone in her family was on Team Liam and looking forward to the wedding.

"The wedding is less than a month away, and there is still so much to do," said Lorraine.

"It's been a year in the making." Liam smashed a tile on the table with a jubilant grin. "I've waited long enough!"

"What's left to do?" asked Dee, studying the line of dominoes. Her eyes narrowed in concentration.

"We're working on the seating arrangements, that's the first fitting, the gifts for the wedding party, discussing plans with the photographer, to name a few," said Lorraine.

"Well, you don't have to worry about the bridal shower. Your mom and I have everything handled. Tomorrow night, you can just sit back and enjoy," said Dee.

"I can make everything a lot easier." Liam pointed a hand to his chest. "Just follow me down to the courthouse. We can be married tomorrow."

"Domino! I'm out." Brandon threw his hands up in the air. "In the words of DJ Khaled, all I do is win!"

Everyone tossed their remaining dominoes to Lorraine, who reluctantly added them up and placed fifty points on the scoreboard for the other team.

As game night wore on, Lorraine stole worried glances in Liam's direction. She couldn't afford to wait much longer to tell him about the job offer. Mr. Holloway had given her one week to express her interest in the senior auditor position. More pressing was the fast-approaching wedding date. She needed to find the right moment to talk to Liam before deciding.

After five games of dominoes, a handful of snack breaks, and several bathroom pauses, Brandon and Dee called it a night. Everyone pitched in to clean up, and soon Liam and Lorraine were alone.

Liam gestured toward the patio. She loved how they'd learned to communicate without saying a word. They each grabbed a jacket and headed outside.

Holding hands, they gazed out at the beautiful Tallahassee moonlight. Laughter and chatter from neighboring homes created a tranquil atmosphere.

Lorraine stared at the twinkling stars as if they would provide encouragement. "I wonder what the temperature will be the day of our wedding?" asked Lorraine.

"Doesn't matter." He looked into her eyes.

Lorraine slipped her hand out of his. The instant he said it didn't matter, she knew he would minimize the situation.

"Did I say something wrong?"

She turned to him. "Liam, I know you mean well, but you're oversimplifying things, and you're minimizing my feelings."

"But it doesn't matter what the weather is like on our wedding day. It will still be the best day of my life."

Lorraine squinted and tilted her head to the side. "What if something goes wrong?"

"Like what?"

"Anything … What if the flowers don't arrive or the pastor gets sick or my dress doesn't fit?"

"Then we'll get married without the flowers, we'll find another preacher, and you'll wear another dress. But we'll get married! That's all that matters."

Lorraine sighed and rolled her eyes.

Deep furrows crept across Liam's forehead. "I'm sorry, honey. I didn't mean to minimize your feelings. It's just that I hate seeing you anxious and overwhelmed. I know how hard you've been working to make this day special. I'm so excited to be your husband, and all I can think about is marrying you as soon as possible. But I know the wedding isn't just about me. It's about us. I can't wait to stand at the altar in front of our friends and family to promise to love you for the rest of my life." He pulled her closer. "Tell me what I can do to make things easier for you."

"Really?"

"Yes. What do you need me to do?"

"I'm going over the guest list with the coordinator on Monday evening. If you could join us, that would be great. She's going to let me know who hasn't responded to the invitations. I'll need your help contacting those people. We want to get an exact head count."

"I'll be there." After a brief pause, he added. "And Lorraine?"

"Yes?"

"In the future, please let me know what you need from me. Give me the opportunity to be your hero. I plan to spend the rest of my life loving you and making your life easier."

Indeed, God had blessed her more than she could have asked for in a man.

He pulled her closer until their lips touched. Lorraine's heart thumped. Butterflies filled her stomach. Then she disappeared into his kiss. She had a man who loved her, a family who supported her, a job she enjoyed, and friends who cared.

Lorraine could no longer keep it from him. She turned to Liam, her expression a blend of excitement and anxiety. "I have some good news to share."

***

Liam took a step back. Her expression sent a different message. If this were good news, why did she look so pessimistic? "What's going on?"

"Remember last year when I applied for the senior auditor position?"

"How could I forget? I helped you study for the exam."

"Yes, you did. The position has reopened. It's mine if I want it. And I don't have to re-take the exam."

Liam's jaws clenched at the mention of the position. After a brief pause, he finally spoke. "That's great."

How's this going to impact our plans to start a family? We just talked about starting a family. Should I bring this up now? She's so happy right now. If I push too hard, I'll ruin this moment for her.

"Liam?" murmured Lorraine.

He drew in a breath and held it. Was he being difficult? This wasn't about him. She was excited. But he couldn't stop the words from plummeting out of his mouth.

"I know this is what you wanted at one time, and I'm proud of you. I just know that this is how couples drift. Too many late nights and missed dinners pulled them in different directions. I don't want that to happen to us."

Lorraine's face tightened, disappointment etched across it. "I don't want that either. That's why I'm fighting for this opportunity and our marriage. Can't we figure out a way instead of having me choose?" Her words hung in the air like the scent of a dead skunk.

Liam's heart wrenched. His own feelings about starting a family unexpectedly mingled with her desire to be successful in her career. He longed for the opportunity to father a child and give the child all the love he didn't receive from his biological father.

"I want to believe we can. But right now, it feels like the job is already winning."

Lorraine looked away, perhaps wanting to avoid his penetrating gaze. After a few moments, she looked at him. "Then help me make sure it doesn't. Don't let fear decide for us."

"I don't know if I can do that. Look, it's getting late and I should probably get going."

He cupped her face in his hands and placed a subtle kiss on her lips. The tension lingered. Even as he walked through the door, Liam's mind played tricks.

Her words were sure when we talked about it days ago. How could she change her mind so quickly? Am I able to trust what she says? Maybe this is a sign of things to come. And if it is, could this be the beginning of the end for us?

Liam stared out the passenger-side window as the car eased out of the parking lot. At the red light, he flicked on the right blinker. He should have been rejoicing with Lorraine. He should have been happy. She deserved every good thing. But this promotion felt mistimed. Some opportunities move us forward; others pull us in another direction entirely.

Chapter 9

Monday night found Liam at the gym with Donnie for their weekly workout. A strenuous workout was just what he needed. A few extra weightlifting reps and a couple of games of basketball seemed to at least relieve some of his stress. Even with his muscles burning, Liam's mind lingered elsewhere.

"You all right?" asked Donnie as they walked to the car an hour later.

"Yes. Sorry to call the workout short, but I promised to meet Lorraine and the wedding planner this evening."

"I get that. Anything I can do to help?" Donnie slid into the passenger seat.

"Just show up with the ring, bro."

Liam climbed in behind the steering wheel, snapped in the seatbelt, and waited for Donnie to do the same. He was halfway home before the silence in the vehicle got the best of him. Their Monday afternoon workouts were usually more spirited, with lots of trash talking. In the summer, when days were longer, spirited banter filled their jogs from the gym to their mother's home. Donnie, also deep in thought, stared out the window.

Liam monitored the road. Each passing well-manicured home sparked thoughts of his ever-increasing dilemmas. The letter from his biological father, wedding plans, Lorraine's promotion, and change of mind about having a baby pounded in his head like a heavy-duty excavator digging dirt and gravel. He had no desire to discuss it.

After a quiet ride home, Liam pulled into their mother's driveway. He remembered how easily she detected when something was not quite right with them. Peeping in the rearview mirror, he pasted a smile on his face before walking through the front door.

"How was your workout?" asked Daisy, rounding the corner from the back of the house.

"Pretty good." Liam leaned in for a quick kiss on the cheek. "I'm gonna jump in the shower. Gotta meet Lorraine later."

Daisy narrowed her eyes and paused before responding. "Okay …"

Liam darted to the back of the house before she could start asking questions. When he returned, hints of onion, garlic, and herbs danced in the air. Daisy sat at the kitchen table; her eyes focused on a crossword puzzle on her iPad screen. Without warning, his stomach released a raucous rumble.

"Your brother had to leave," said Daisy, looking up from her tablet. "I made a to-go plate for him to take home. Would you like something to eat before you leave?"

Growl!

Betrayed by his gut once again, Liam conceded, "Thanks, Mom. That would be great. I'll grab it."

Liam scooped a heap of lasagna onto a plate, grabbed a glass of sweet tea, and sat across from his mother. "What are you doing tonight? Is Zeke on his way over?"

"Yes. We're planning a quiet evening with a movie." She giggled and then let him bless the food.

"I'm not so young, and I don't know if anyone says that at all." Liam placed a forkful of pasta in his mouth, then looked away.

Daisy leaned back in the chair, her hands gripping a glass of sweet tea as she searched his face. "So, what's on your mind?"

"Not much. Why?" he asked, pretending to examine the food on his plate.

"Is something going on at work that I should know about?" she asked, her voice soft with concern.

"Of course not. After that incident last year, I promised to be transparent about business matters, and that's what I'm doing," said Liam determinedly. He placed another gob of lasagna in his mouth.

"Then what is it?" Daisy turned her tablet over and set it aside.

She's going to keep pushing until I tell her something.

"Is it Lorraine? Does she want you to be more involved with the wedding planning?"

"Yes, she does. That's what I'm doing tonight. Working on the unanswered RSVPs." Liam took a couple of swallows of tea.

"Glad to hear it."

He waited for his mother's next question. When she had no more questions, he said, "Lorraine received a promotion offer at work."

"That's great," Daisy leaned back, smiling. "You must be very proud of her."

Liam forced a smile. "I am. But the timing is all wrong?"

"Says who?" she asked, switching to a cynical tone.

Liam placed his fork on the plate, leaned back, and crossed his arms. "We were planning on starting a family right away."

"What's the rush?" Daisy took a sip of tea.

"No rush, I guess. But we'd already talked about it. She changed her mind without telling me."

"Un-huh." Daisy's troubled eyes sliced into him. He could feel her concern.

Liam shrugged his shoulders. "Go ahead. Don't hold back, Mom. I know you have more to say."

"You're a grown man, and I can't tell you what to do. But I will warn you not to pressure her. Hear her out."

"I don't get it," said Liam, raising both hands in the air. "We had a plan. She gave her perspective, and I gave mine. We developed a timeline, and we agreed to start a family right away."

"Sounds more like a business meeting to me."

She had a point. He was methodical in decision-making. It involved setting goals, creating a plan, and acting. The process allowed him to respond and not react to everyday roadblocks. Having his mother say what he already knew did little to cut the disappointment. Despite their disagreement, he wanted to hear Lorraine's point of view.

Liam glanced at the clock. He stuffed the last few bites of food into his mouth. "Thanks for the lasagna. I should go." He stood, rinsed his plate and glass, and then placed them in the dishwasher.

"Tell Lorraine hello for me."

"I will. Thank you for listening, Mom. And thanks for the advice." He walked over to Daisy and gently hugged her.

She smiled. "That's what moms are for. I love you."

"Love you, too."

He walked out of the house, climbed inside his vehicle, and closed the door. Talking with his mother was excellent therapy. Liam put the car in gear, thrusting thoughts of babies and bio-dads from his mind. Helping with the wedding was the only thing he could offer, and it was the only thing he could control.

***

Lorraine moved quickly through her condominium, wiping down surfaces, putting away dishes, and fluffing pillows. A vanilla-scented candle filled the atmosphere with the aroma of freshly baked cookies—the sugary scent blended with the faint citrusy hints of the cleaning wipes she used to tidy up.

She pulled a fresh charcuterie board from the refrigerator. A simple but elegant tray she'd picked up at Publix on her way home from work. The crackers jostled when she placed the tray on the dining table. She rearranged the treats with ease, though her thoughts were anything but settled.

Each passing moment triggered thoughts of her increasing concerns. The wedding plans, the promotion, and Liam's letter from his biological father weighed heavily on her mind. But she carried on, arranging snacks, utensils, and drinks on the table as if compartmentalizing her worries.

The doorbell rang. She hurried to the entrance, finding her mother waiting on the other side.

"Hey, Mom." She smiled, relieving Helen of the cake dish. "You didn't have to bring anything. But I'm glad you did."

"I wasn't sure if you had time to prepare something to snack on, so I made a pound cake. I hope you don't mind." Helen followed Lorraine to the kitchen.

"This is perfect. I was in a hurry, so I bought a charcuterie board. But I know everyone will love your homemade pound cake. You always know what to do."

Lorraine placed the cake carrier on the counter. The vintage Tupperware container with a sturdy base, domed lid, and flexible gold straps was a treasured family item. "I remember this cake carrier from when I was a little girl. You used it whenever there was a potluck or something at the church. And you always got it back at the end of the event."

"That's right. And I want it back when you're done with it, too." Helen chuckled. "It may be old, but it sure is sturdy. It's just like me."

Lorraine snuck a peek to see if her mother was wearing the hearing aids. Satisfied that the devices were in, she replied, "You're not old, Mom."

"Tell that to my body." Helen looked around the room. "What do you need me to do?"

"Everything is done. But I'd like to talk to you about something. We have a few minutes before the others arrive."

"Sure. Is everything okay?"

"I want your advice about something."

Moving to the living room, Lorraine sat on the couch with her hands folded in her lap. She turned slightly toward her mother, who sat next to her, body angled in a way that said I'm listening.

Gathering her thoughts, Lorraine looked into her mother's eyes, which peered back with years of experience and wisdom. A trace of a smile softened the corners of Helen's lips, but her expression remained pensive.

She exhaled and finally said, "Do you remember the promotion I didn't get last year?"

Helen tilted her head. "Yes, I do."

"They offered it to me." Her voice quivered, and she felt her mother's hand rest tenderly on hers, an unspoken quiet reassurance.

"That's fantastic. But why do you look so sad?" Helen's eyebrows lifted as if she could sense there was more to the story.

"Liam and I … we talked about starting a family after the wedding. We agreed I would take a leave of absence to stay home with the baby. It wouldn't be right for me to take the position and then take a leave of absence to start a family. I must choose one or the other." She met her mother's gaze. "What do you think I should do? Would it be selfish to accept the position instead of starting our family?"

Helen didn't answer immediately. She held Lorraine's gaze, her expression unreadable, as if pondering her words. But there was no judgment, just patience.

"What do you think?" asked Helen.

Lorraine tilted her head to one side. "Part of me thinks it's selfish because Liam and I agreed on starting a family right away. But that was before the position became available."

Helen raised an index finger. "Here's the thing: after the two of you are married, life won't be just about what you want or what he wants. It'll be about what's best for the marriage."

"We're not married yet."

"Exactly," Helen leaned in slightly. "But you have led him to believe certain things would happen after the wedding. If you have changed your mind or are thinking about it, now is the time to tell him. It impacts his life as well as yours."

"I told him, and then things got awkward. That was Friday night. Haven't seen him since. Talked to him twice on the phone, but the conversations were terse. He's supposed to join us tonight." Lorraine looked off into the distance. "Unless he changes his mind."

"Then you should find the right time and the right place to discuss it with him. If you can't be honest with each other now, you won't be honest with each other after the wedding."

"What if it is a dealbreaker for Liam?" Lorraine held her hand over her heart.

"Have you prayed about it?"

Lorraine gave her mother the side-eye. She'd expected the response. "No, I haven't. But I'm going to."

"And after you pray about it, discuss it with your fiancé. He can make his own decision about something that will affect his future."

Lorraine knew that praying about the situation was the right thing to do. It wasn't the prayer that caused her anxiety; it was God's answer that worried her. Was she prepared to do what God instructed her to do?

If they hadn't offered her the promotion, there wouldn't be a problem. But they offered it. And she'd made plans to start a family with Liam, and that made her happy. Lorraine always gave more than was required in any situation. And this was no different. She wanted to excel in her career and at motherhood. The question was whether she would have to choose one over the other.

Minutes later, Lorraine's phone rang just as there was a knock at the door.

"Answer your phone", said Helen, smiling. "It's Liam, I recognize the ringtone. I'll get the door."

"Thanks, Mom." Lorraine turned her attention to her cell.

"Hey, babe. Are you on your way?" she answered, playing along with their pretend-nothing's-wrong game.

"Yes. Finished my workout with Donnie and had a bite to eat with Mom. Don't worry, I showered," he teased.

"Great. Mom is here, and Bri just walked through the door."

"See you soon. I love you."

"Love you, too." Lorraine ended the call.

"Everything okay over there?" asked Helen.

"Yes, ma'am. Liam's on his way." Lorraine turned her attention to the wedding planner, who was sitting at the table. "Sorry about that, Bri. How are you?"

"Fantastic! How is the bride-to-be? It's getting close. This time next month, you'll be Mrs. Liam Whittington. Are you excited?" asked Bri, her words flowing like a waterfall with no pauses for breath.

"I'm great. Thanks for asking. And, yes, I'm excited." Lorraine pulled her in for an embrace.

Bri smiled and took her seat. "I know I'm a little early, so we have time to wait for Liam before we get started. He doesn't need to rush on my account."

Lorraine waved a hand. "He ought to be here within ten minutes."

"Awesome, I have time to finish eating your mom's pound cake. Didn't expect to be treated with dessert. Mrs. Davis, I'd love the recipe if you don't mind sharing. My aunt bakes all the time, but she doesn't like to share the recipes. Are you like that? I mean, if you are, I respect your choice." Bri spoke in rapid-fire sentences again, words flying so quickly they seemed to require a speed limit.

Helen let out a soft laugh. "So glad you like it. I'd be happy to share the recipe."

Bri took a bite of cake and swallowed. She reached for her laptop. "Thank you. If you dictate it to me, I'll type it in my notes. Don't you love technology? There's an app for everything. There's even an app that tells me when it's time to breathe. Can you believe that?"

Lorraine listened to her mother share the recipe, but her mind wandered to the promotion offer and all the benefits that came along with it. A tap on the door interrupted her musing. She bounced to the front door and pulled it open. Liam was standing there. Their eyes met, and his gaze quickened her pulse. Even in their current state of disagreement, there was something about him she couldn't resist.

She didn't think, just reached for him and kissed him. "Hey, babe. Glad you're here."

"Me, too," he said, stepping in with a warm, calm smile.

"Everything okay?" she asked.

"Sure." He scratched his head. Lorraine could tell he didn't want to talk about it.

"Mrs. Davis, you look lovely. It's nice to see you again." Liam greeted.

"Good to see you, too." Helen rose from her seat to embrace her future son-in-law.

"Hello, Bri. Thanks for meeting with us," he said, placing a soft tap on her shoulder.

"No problem. I'm here for you guys. Besides, I work all hours of the day. You can catch me on my computer late at night. You can catch me working in the wee hours of the morning. So, are you getting excited? Countdown to the big day!" Bri sang the last portion of her barrage of statements before taking a breath.

Liam raised an eyebrow in his fiancée's direction. "More than you know."

Lorraine cocked her head toward Liam. "We have a charcuterie board, and Mom made a pound cake. What would you like?"

Liam rubbed his hands together. "A thick slice of your mom's pound cake, of course."

"That's my boy." Helen smiled, pushing back from the table. "Wash your hands, and I'll cut a big slice for you."

"What would you like to drink?" asked Lorraine.

"Water, please."

Liam washed and dried his hands at the sink and slid into a chair at the table. Helen placed the cake and a glass of water in front of him. He blessed the food.

"Bri, do you mind if I eat while we work?" he asked after taking a generous bite and chasing it with a sip of water.

"Not at all. Let's get started." Bri positioned her iPad in front of her and tapped in a few commands. "It looks like around twenty percent of the invitations are unanswered. But don't be concerned. I mean, I know you are concerned, but twenty percent is about average."

"So, what do we do?" asked Lorraine.

"Glad you asked." Bri giggled. "First, take a deep breath. I suggest you call them. Calmly let them know you haven't received the RSVP, then ask if they will attend. If you can't reach them by phone, follow up with a text message or email. I can email the list to each of you if you prefer."

"Why don't you send it to me?" Lorraine suggested. "I'll extract the names from Liam's guest list and send them to him."

Liam nodded. "Great idea."

"If you send me some names from your list, Lorraine, I'll make a few calls too," said Helen. "I can set a fire under my sister, Winnie, and her crew better than you can. Besides, I know how busy you get with work and all."

"Your mom's right," Bri said to Lorraine. "You're the only person I know who works more hours than I do."

The front door flew open, and Dee stood manipulating her wheeled suitcase over the threshold. "Hey, everybody."

"Let me help you with that." Liam sprang from his seat and took the luggage from her, rolling it inside.

"Thank you. Would you put it in a corner somewhere?" Dee walked to the couch and slumped clumsily onto it. "I love the travel to out-of-town worksites, but boy, am I exhausted."

"I was just commenting about how much Lorraine works. I guess that goes for you as well. I mean, you guys do work at the same place." Bri frowned.

Dee shook her head. "From what I hear, Lorraine might work a lot more soon."

Lorraine gave Dee a not-now look with crumpled lips, creased eyebrows, and her head angled to one side.

"Or not!" Dee's eyes danced toward Bri. "What can I do to help with the wedding plans?"

Lorraine coerced a smile, but her stomach curled as she noticed the flash of tension in Liam's jaw. He didn't say a word, just kept his attention on Bri's notes, his grip tight on the pen.

Dee moved on, chatting with her mother about floral arrangements, but Lorraine couldn't rid the notion that the moment they were alone, Liam would have plenty to say. The question wasn't whether he'd bring it up; it was when and how much damage it would do.

***

"Good night, Mrs. Davis." Liam's eyes focused on his future mother-in-law, but his thoughts were on what Dee had said earlier: "From what I hear, Lorraine might work a lot more soon."

"Bye, Mom. Let me know when you get home." Lorraine pulled her mother in for a last hug. Helen slid into the driver's seat of her car and closed the door. The couple watched as she drove away.

It'd taken longer than expected for everyone to leave. Liam would have asked everyone to leave about an hour earlier if it were up to him. But it wasn't his place to dismiss anyone.

Bri was the first to go, reviewing their assigned tasks before saying goodnight. Then, Dee, who had been yawning throughout most of the meeting, headed to her bedroom. Lorraine's mother insisted on tidying the kitchen before she left.

"Let's sit in the living room. I'll grab some water from the fridge," said Lorraine when they stepped back inside the condo.

Liam sat on the edge of the couch, staring at nothing. The words he needed to say sat heavy in his heart. He wondered how she could change her mind about the plans they had made for the future. Wasn't she looking forward to starting a family with him? He wanted to be supportive, but he couldn't help being selfish.

Lorraine returned with two bottles of water and plopped onto the couch next to him. Liam opened the water bottle, lifted it to his lips, and took a sip.

"So, when were you going to tell me you already decided about the promotion?" His words tumbled out swiftly and unsteadily like a house of cards collapsing in haste once he started. There was no stopping the cascade.

Lorraine tilted an eyebrow. "What are you talking about? What makes you think I've decided?"

He shook his head.

Lorraine scowled. "I told you it was an opportunity I couldn't ignore."

He was pensive for a moment before saying, "And when I told you my concerns, you brushed them off! You made your choice, and it wasn't me. You didn't choose us."

"Are you asking me to choose between love and ambition?"

Liam hated this. Never in a million years did he think they would have this discussion.

He hesitated. She'd asked a valid question. "Of course not!"

"Would you still want to marry me if I took the job?" If her eyes could shoot lasers, she would have burned him into pieces by now, so he measured his words and softened his tone.

"You know my history. I've always been upfront with you about wanting to be a father. I don't want to miss the opportunity to create a family like the one my adoptive parents created for me."

Lorraine took his hand and pulled him onto the couch. She stared into his eyes. He sensed his heartbeat racing.

"I get that. I want a family, too. But I'm afraid I'll lose myself if I don't explore this opportunity before starting a family."

Liam groaned as if he hated hearing her concern. He didn't like it. Lorraine had agreed they'd start a family right away. He knew he was being selfish. He wanted to marry Lorraine and have her as the mother of his children. But if she chose her career now, how was he to know she wouldn't always choose her career over family? He thought they were growing something solid together, like a tree establishing roots. But now it felt like she was plucking it out of the ground before it flourished.

Now he was not only confused but also angry. *After everything we've been through together, the secrets shared, the love promised, and the future hopes, why would she accept the position without discussing it with me? This decision has implications not only for Lorraine but also for me and our future family.*

Lorraine positioned her arms across her chest. Her shoulders rose and then she dropped them, as if she had finished carrying the conversation's weight. "I don't have the energy to beg you to see me. I think it's time for you to leave."

"So that's it. I disagree with you, and suddenly I don't see you?" Liam's voice dropped as he said it. He didn't mean to sound so angry. But maybe anger was easier than the ache.

"Look, I don't know how to fix this. But walking out feels like the worst thing to do."

He didn't move.

Lorraine stared with no response.

"Fine. If you want me to go, I'll go."

There was nothing more to say without making it worse. So, he walked to the door as if his heart wasn't breaking into pieces.

Chapter 10

That night, Liam went twelve rounds with his dreams. Every time he fell asleep, another nightmare came swinging. Like a boxer slipping punches, the visions landed hit after hit. The image of a strange man standing at his mother's doorstep wouldn't let him rest. The unwelcome visitor tried to force his way into the house to harm his mother. Liam threw several punches at the man, but the visitor ducked, weaved, and just wouldn't quit. Although he did not know what Curtis Barnes looked like, Liam was sure the man at the door was his biological father.

The next round of nightmares included visions of an angry Lorraine standing at the front door. In the dream, he fought a strong tornado-like wind trying to yank her away from him. With all his might, Liam tried to pull her into his arms. But the winds were too strong, and for every two inches he pulled her in, the winds snatched her back four inches. Soon, she was almost out of his grip. It was a knockout night. Bad dreams battered his psyche until his alarm finally rang on Tuesday morning.

"Good morning, son. How did you sleep?" His mother asked when he entered the kitchen in pursuit of coffee. Daisy sat at the table with a cup of coffee and her iPad, reading her morning Scripture.

"Good morning. All right, I guess," he said with a yawn. Liam placed a pod in the Keurig and pressed the start button. Then he walked over to his mother and brushed a soft kiss across her forehead.

"What's the matter?"

How does she do that? She can always tell when something's wrong.

His mother's God-given intuition bothered him because it made him feel exposed. But today, he was grateful because he wanted — no, he needed to talk to his mother about the Lorraine dream.

The Keurig purred, jarring him from his thoughts. "I can't shake this dream."

His mother's eyes widened. "Do you want to talk about it?"

"It was about Lorraine. But it wasn't pleasant." He waited for the coffee machine to finish and sat opposite his mother at the table.

"Go on." She leaned forward in her chair.

Liam filled her in on his dream of the tornado pulling Lorraine away from him.

"I see." She raised her cup to her lips for a sip. "You know, in the Scriptures, God often encouraged people or gave them a warning in a dream. Like Joseph's brothers bowing down to him as sheaves of grain in Genesis. Or when God spoke to Abimelech to warn him about his actions, also in Genesis."

Liam raised the cup to his mouth, realized the coffee was too hot, and returned it to the table in front of him. "You think God is warning me about something?"

"What do you think?" She asked, staring at him.

Liam nervously cleared his throat. "I don't know, maybe God is warning me that something could pull Lorraine away from me. Last night, Lorraine and I argued about her job offer. She seems to think she'll lose herself if she doesn't explore the opportunity."

Daisy shot him a sideways glance. "Why does the possibility of her promotion bother you so much?"

"I want to experience the bond between father and child. I want the joy of building a loving family like you and Dad did. What if she changes her mind and never wants to have children?" He sipped his coffee.

"Have you voiced your concerns to Lorraine?"

"She knows I want to be a father."

Daisy slightly tilted her head, shifting her eyes toward him. "What has Lorraine said or done to make you think she may never want to have children?"

"Nothing, really." Liam sipped his coffee and leaned forward.

"Did you ask her about it?"

He hesitated. The answer to that question was no.

"Every time the subject comes up, an argument ensues. It's better not to talk about it." Liam waved off the suggestion.

Daisy glanced at him and nodded questioningly. "Honey, you can't just not talk about it. Don't you trust her to tell you the truth about her feelings?"

"I don't know anymore. I trusted her when she said she wanted to start a family right away." Liam raised a hand and swiped his face with it before taking a sip of coffee.

"What is a marriage without trust?" she asked.

He recognized the worried look in her eyes. His mother had always been straightforward with him. There was no reason for her to stop now.

As much as Liam hated to admit it, his mother was right. He needed to talk to Lorraine.

Thirty minutes later, they left the table with Liam thanking his mother for listening. Daisy smiled and promised to always be there, and Liam knew she spoke the truth.

***

Liam hopped into his car and headed to work with plenty on his mind. As usual, his mother made sense, and he needed to talk with Lorraine. He tried to call her twice on the way to work. But she hadn't answered. When he pulled in front of the office, he tried one last time.

"Hello?" she answered, her voice even but cautious.

Liam released a flicker of a smile and took a deep breath before responding. "Lorraine, thanks for picking up. I think we should talk."

"So do I. I'm sorry I didn't pick up before; I just needed some time to think."

He pressed his forehead to the steering wheel for a moment. "I understand. I'm sorry for the way I left things last night."

"Me, too," said Lorraine.

An uncomfortable silence fell between them.

"I hate it when we fight," she said.

"So do I. I tossed and turned all night. I know how much the promotion means to you. I was there last year when you applied the first time. And I want you to know I'm proud of you. But ..."

"But what?"

"But I don't want this to come between us." Liam flailed his hands in the air as if she could see him.

"I keep thinking about our vision of starting a family, a home, building something steady together. That's what I thought we both wanted."

"We are. But my career is part of that, Liam. I don't want it to sound like two competing dreams. It's in the future. I just see more than one way to get there."

"But it feels like our paths are separating. Like you're running after this opportunity, and I'm standing here holding onto the plan we already made. I don't know where they meet anymore." Liam hunched his shoulders and shook his head.

"They meet with us. Always with us. Why does it sound like you're questioning that?" Lorraine lowered her voice to almost a whisper, like she was afraid of the answer.

"Because I'm afraid, Lorraine. Afraid that if we're already tugging in different directions before the wedding, we'll drift further as life gets harder."

"So, what are you saying? That one of us must let go of the dream, or we can't move forward?" asked Lorraine, her tone laced with weariness.

The line went silent for a beat, only the faint sound of Lorraine breathing on the other end.

"I don't know. I don't want to lose us before we've even begun." He didn't want to argue with her. It made him angry that she was making plans for a promotion instead of focusing on what they'd discussed about their future. It should carry way more weight with her than anything a job could offer.

"Maybe it's something we should discuss with the therapist present. We have an appointment scheduled."

She was right; the therapist often helped them develop communication techniques. Maybe she could help with this issue. "I think that would work."

"I know we are supposed to have dinner tonight. But …

As angry as he was with her, Liam still longed to be in her presence. "I want to have dinner. Will you still join me?"

"Only if you make a promise."

Liam sank back into the seat and dropped his shoulders. "What's that?"

"That we keep the topic of my promotion off limits until we meet with the therapist," said Lorraine.

He closed his eyes for a split second. "I can do that. Pick you up at seven?"

"Make it seven thirty and you have a date."

***

After his emotional phone call with Lorraine, Liam's morning seemed to go from bad to worse. He spent the better part of the morning on the phone attempting to secure approval for an upcoming tree removal project. Work on the E&G contract could not begin without the permit. A delay would cause the project to be pushed to the following week. But the forecast called for heavy rain, which would make the work even harder.

"No. I don't want to be transferred again!" Liam repeatedly banged his fist against the desk. "You have my completed application for the tree removal. The tree inspector found that the tree complied with Tallahassee's land development code; you have the documentation. I don't know what we're waiting on."

Liam and the other person on the other end of the phone were both irritated.

"I understand your frustration, sir. But there is nothing we can do at this point. Like I said before, perhaps someone in the growth management department could assist you."

Liam pushed his chair away from the desk and stood. Every muscle in his face tightened as if he were about to throw a punch. "I spoke with them earlier, and they transferred me to your department. So, no thank you."

Liam disconnected the call and started pacing the room. "Unbelievable! Government bureaucracy. Duplication of effort. No one knows what the other one is doing." Every word punctuated with a heavy foot to the floor or a tight fist in the air.

Sophia's voice disrupted his frenzy. "Mr. Whittington?"

"Yes?" He wondered if she had heard his ranting.

"There's a Curtis Barnes on line one for you."

Just hearing his biological father's name said out loud caused him to freeze in place. He stood dumbfounded for a moment.

This man is crazy. He has the audacity to call my place of business! I shouldn't talk to him, but I want to give him a piece of my mind.

"Mr. Whittington, are you there?"

"Yes, I'm here. Thank you, Sophia. You can transfer the call."

He planted himself in the chair like a man about to go to war with a phone as his weapon. "Mr. Barnes, how can I help you?"

"Good morning, son," said Curtis, sounding light, practiced, almost rehearsed.

An uneasy silence fell over the line. Liam was not about to respond to this stranger calling him son. Only Harold or Daisy Whittington could use the moniker. This man had not earned the right.

"I wasn't sure if you received my letter."

"I received the letter."

Another chasm of silence.

"I understand your anger and concern," said Curtis. "You don't know me. But I thought maybe we could get to know each other. Why don't you come see me? Like I said in the letter, I'm at Motel 6 on Apalachee."

The outlandish request added fuel to the fire.

"Not going to happen." Liam flung his head back and rolled his eyes.

"Then maybe we'll meet at the wedding."

Liam sprang from his chair like a lion ready to attack. "That would be a mistake," he said, accentuating his words with an angry finger jabbing the air.

"Would it? Because I got some things you need to hear. But if you'd rather have me air it out in front of your little bride, your adopted mother, and all your guests, I can do that, too."

"Keep my bride and my mother out of this. Besides, if you had anything worth saying, you would've said it in that letter. Instead, you're playing games, trying to force me into a meeting I don't want. You will not manipulate me.

"Just listen."

Liam's chest rose and fell. "No. You listen. My wedding is not your opportunity to enter my life. If you show up, security will escort you out. If you try to cause a scene, you'll regret it."

"You're acting all high and mighty. You're no better than I am. Watch and see. In a few years, you'll be just like me. No kids, no wife, and no family."

"This conversation is over. Stay away from my wedding. Stay out of my life."

Liam disconnected the call. He was so angry he could hear his heart pumping out of his chest.

This man is a nutcase. But he's messing with the wrong one now. He is interrupting my life and claiming a position in my family like he earned it.

Click, click, click.

He heard footsteps approaching.

Glancing at his watch, he thought, *That's probably Mom. I'd better fix my face. Don't want to give her a reason to pry.*

"Hi, Liam." Daisy opened the door and peeped in without knocking.

"Hi, Mom," he said, carefully controlling his tone.

She smiled. "I just wanted to let you know I'm here."

"I'm glad you're here," he said, shutting down the computer. "I need to run a quick errand."

"Great. I've got it from here." Daisy turned and walked away.

Liam dropped his shoulders as relief settled into his bones. He snatched his keys and phone off the desk and headed out the door.

Chapter 11

Curtis looked at the phone like it was Mike Tyson biting off his ear. Then he ripped the receiver from the cradle and flung it across the room. The coiled cord jerked the handset in midair. It smacked against the nightstand and dangled. The base slid, teetered an inch, and then fell—the phone's off-the-hook warning shrilled throughout the silence in the room. In rhythm, the red message light blinked.

Desperate to calm his nerves, he groped in his pockets for a cigarette. Finding nothing, he rummaged through the drawer for a fresh pack.

"Look what you made me do, son," Curtis mumbled as he tore open the cellophane wrapper. "What did you expect? I reached out. I tried, and you spat it back in my face. You pushed me. You're just like everyone else, thinking you're better than me. If you can't handle a little truth, that's on you, not me."

In one angry motion, he opened the lid and removed the foil from the cigarette pack. He retrieved one and lit it. "They probably poisoned you and Donnie to be against me." *Of course, y'all hate me; that's what they wanted. Now I look like the bad guy while Harold and Daisy Whittington look like saints. They probably told you I was worthless. That's not the truth. You don't even realize they brainwashed you.*

Looking into the cloudy mirror over the dresser, he raised an eyebrow in disbelief before taking a drag. "At least I took the time to write a letter. An actual letter. I put myself out there, and this is the thanks I get? Disrespect! Man, you should be grateful I even tried. If anybody should be mad, it's me. I'm your blood. I deserve the respect."

Curtis slammed a palm against the dresser. "My son had the nerve to hang up on me!"

He began pacing. The sound of traffic roared from the nearby parkway, and a door slammed in the distance. "But you know what? *That's fine. You're still my son, whether you like it or not. I'll just call in for reinforcements, that's all. Then you'll see who I really am. Then you'll realize the lies they've been feeding you and your brother.*

Chapter 12

Donnie's front door flew open before Liam could ring the doorbell. He stood barefoot in pajama pants and a FAMU Theatre T-shirt. Liam entered the foyer and followed him into the central living area and dining space. A half-read manuscript sat on the coffee table; a tall ring light glowed in the corner.

Donnie's eyes scanned Liam's face and held his palms up. "What's the emergency?"

Liam pulled an envelope from his back pocket before sitting on the jewel-toned sofa. "There's a situation I wanted to discuss with you."

Donnie sat across from him on the baroque chair. "What's going on? You said little on the phone. Is Mom okay?"

"She's fine."

"What's that?" asked Donnie, pointing to the envelope in his brother's hand.

Liam scooted closer to the edge of the chair and leaned in. "It's a letter from Curtis Barnes, our biological father."

Donnie's eyes widened for a millisecond before he coerced them back to neutral. His lips separated as if to speak, but no words came out. Liam recognized confusion flickering in his eyes.

"Did you get a letter?"

Donnie shook his head. "No, I didn't."

Liam watched silently as Donnie opened the envelope and read the letter.

"Can you believe the nerve of this guy?" Donnie released a somber chuckle.

Donnie held the letter at arm's length as if it were physically repulsive. "This? This is a script. And it's not even a good one."

He tossed the document on the living room table before asking, "Did you do it?"

"Do what?"

"Meet him at the hotel?"

Liam threw his palm up hard. "No. And I hadn't planned on doing so until he called the office this morning, with threats of disrupting my wedding."

Liam sprang to his feet and wandered to the other side of the room before stopping to rest against the wall next to the *Raisin in the Sun* poster.

"What? Is he planning on walking into the wedding like we're in a Tyler Perry reunion movie? That will not happen!" Donnie flailed his hands in the air. "Where is all of this coming from? The man has never reached out to us before. Why did he suddenly write to you?"

"He says he has something I need to hear."

Donnie laughed in disbelief. "The only thing I want to hear is why he chose a life that did not include caring for his sons."

"I don't even care about that. I don't want to upset Lorraine on the one day she's been waiting for all her life. And I especially don't want to upset Mom. She knows nothing about this, and I plan to keep it that way." Liam balled his fist. He felt like punching the wall.

Donnie nodded. "You're right. She and Dad are the only parents we've ever known."

"They poured love into us from the moment they became our parents and never made us feel anything less than their sons," said Liam.

"When do you plan on meeting him?"

"No time like the present," said Liam, jaw tight and nostrils flaring. He snatched the keys from his pants pocket.

"Give me a second to put on some clothes, and I'm ready to roll," said Donnie, exiting the room with a venomous laugh.

***

Twenty-five minutes later, Liam's SUV rolled past the bright blue sign with a large, striking red number six in the center. A few people stood outside the building, some in pajamas, while others walked toward a nearby gas station.

Donnie pointed to one of the bright blue doors on the second floor. "That is his room."

Liam parked at the far end of the lot. The two stared straight ahead for a moment. Their focus was fixed on the door marked 249.

"So, what's the plan?" asked Donnie.

"First," said Liam, taking a deep breath. "We don't go inside. If he wants to talk, he can do it outside. Other than that, there is no plan. Let's hear what he has to say and get on with the rest of our lives." Liam spat the words like they were irrelevant. But deep down, he knew this day would be a pivotal one. Before and after meeting his biological father would define the rest of his life.

"You know Mom would tell us to pray before we get out of the car," said Donnie.

Liam scoffed, unable to keep the frustration out of his voice. He was the big brother. He should have been the one to suggest prayer. But deep inside, he feared God would want him to have compassion for Curtis. And he wasn't ready to do that. "Yes, she would. But …"

"But nothing," Donnie interrupted. "We don't know what we're about to face? We need to pray."

A surge of anger rushed through Liam's body. "What are you talking about? Nothing this man has to say will change anything for me."

"Aren't you a little curious about why they gave us up for adoption?"

"Don't care," Liam shook his head. "Just glad they did."

"Either way, I think we should pray before we go any further."

Liam curled his bottom lip in and bit it. "Okay. Go ahead."

"Heavenly Father, please go before us. We don't know what this meeting is about, but You do. Prepare our hearts and minds for what lies ahead. In Jesus' name, amen."

Liam had to admit that despite his feelings about Curtis, he felt better having prayed before exiting the vehicle. Together they marched toward the building and up the stairs like an army of two going into battle.

Pausing in front of room 249, Donnie glanced at his brother. "You ready?" he asked.

"Ready as I'll ever be. Let's get this over with."

Liam pounded three sharp, clipped blows on the door.

"Who is it?" answered a booming voice from the other side of the door.

Liam squared his shoulders and clenched his hands at his side. "Liam and Donnie."

A moment of silence, then loud footsteps bellowed from the other side of the door. Another moment of silence. Perhaps an opportunity for Curtis to check through the peephole. The door swung open, revealing a man who was roughly six feet, three inches tall.

"My boys!" he barked with a wide, welcoming smile. "Come on in." Each word left a trail of old smoke and morning bitterness.

Liam's muscles twitched as the physical resemblance landed like a punch in his gut. They shared the same dark-chocolate complexion and big, round eyes. He took a slow, measured breath.

Time seemed to stand still as they stood perplexed. This stranger, whom they'd just met, behaved as if he were welcoming his long-lost sons home again.

Liam pointed a sharp finger in Curtis' direction. "We're not your boys, and we'd prefer it if you stepped outside."

"Oh, it's like that. Do you think I'm going to harm my own sons?" A sinister grin crept across Curtis' face.

"Why not?" asked Liam, terrifying in its restraint. "You've already threatened me!"

"You mean about the wedding? It worked. I had to get you over here."

"You can say whatever you need to say out here."

"Okay, okay. I get it. Let me grab a smoke first." Curtis backed into the room with a silly grin on his face. With the door open, he grabbed a cigarette and a lighter from the nightstand. After giving the room a quick glance, he stepped outside, and closed the door. Leaning against the wall, he lit a cigarette, glanced from Liam to Donnie, and grinned.

"What information do you have?" asked Liam, getting straight to the point.

Curtis threw his hand up in the air. "Whoa! I'll get to that. Let's catch up first." He took a long drag of the cigarette.

Donnie scrubbed a hand across his face.

"We know all we need to know about you," blurted Liam.

Curtis shook his head. "Well, I been keeping up with the two of you. I must've done something right. Your mama would be proud. God rest her soul."

Donnie adjusted his weight. His eyes held no kindness, zeroing in on Curtis like a hunter waiting for the right moment. "Our mother is proud of us. She tells us every day."

"We aren't here for the small talk. If you have something to say, say it now. Or we're out of here!" Liam snapped, every word purposeful, sharp, and charged with resentment.

Curtis propped one foot against the wall behind him. He held the cigarette with a relaxed grip, lifting it to his mouth in an unhurried movement. A smirk lingered at the corner of his lips as he blew out a thick cloud of smoke. Unbothered and controlled. "I see. They've filled your head with some nonsense. Whatever they told you about me was a lie."

The smug grin stretched across Curtis' face, causing Liam's blood to boil. He clenched and unclenched his fists with restless energy. If he didn't leave soon, Curtis would lose a few teeth.

"What are you talking about?" asked Donnie.

"What'd they tell you about how they got you?" Curtis took another drag.

Donnie fired a sideways glance. "We're not here to answer your questions."

An awkward pause ensued.

Curtis gazed into the distance with pensive eyes. "Your mama didn't know what she was doing when she signed those papers. By then, I was in prison. His posture drooped, lost in whatever thought the smoke carried away. "She was a beautiful woman back in the day."

Donnie turned to Liam. "Let's go. This is foolishness!"

Curtis tossed the cigarette onto the floor, grinding it beneath his shoe. "Harold and Daisy Whittington weren't as upright as you seem to think they were."

Liam jammed his fist into his palm and locked eyes with Curtis.

"Keep my parent's names out of your mouth!" His words bounced off the hard exterior of the second-floor walkway, his tone shrill against the concrete walls and metal railings.

"I guess I hit a nerve," Curtis sneered. "Your perfect parents stole you. They stole both of you."

The words cut through Liam like a freshly sharpened knife. His fury reached a climax. He grabbed Curtis' collar and shoved him up against the wall. "That's a lie!"

Donnie grabbed Liam's wrist, pulling with all his might, trying to break the hold. "Liam, let him go! He's not worth it. We know it's a lie. He knows it's a lie. Don't let him control how this goes."

Finally, Liam freed Curtis. The two stared each other down. After catching his breath, Curtis released a grin so cynical it made Liam take a step back.

"Look, I'm not the bad guy here. They stole you!"

Liam huffed. "What's your motive here? What do you want?"

"An invitation to the wedding. That's all I'm asking."

"Not gonna happen," said Liam.

"Then I'll just show up, anyway. And then I'll let everyone at the wedding know just how sneaky Harold and Daisy Whittington really were."

Liam swung his fist forward. The air swooshed with the promise of impact until Donnie pulled him back with force. If it had not been for his brother's quick reflexes, Curtis would have been lying flat on the concrete walkway.

"Let's go," said Donnie, prodding his brother away from the scene.

"I want my invitation just like every other member of the family!" Yelled Curtis.

"You are not my family!" Liam's blood seethed as they turned and walked toward the stairwell. His head pounded when he thought of all the ways he could hurt or maim Curtis. He vowed to make Curtis regret having returned to Tallahassee.

Chapter 13

My boy is strong! No doubt about it. Curtis' eyes burned with pride. *Like I used to be back when I worked the meat market, hauling sides of beef off the hooks in the freezer.*

He yanked the dingy t-shirt from his body and moved to the grimy mirror. The dim lighting blurred his image as he checked for discoloration. There were no signs of bruising, but he prepared himself for possible soreness in the morning.

He sighed with disappointment, thinking of their first visit with his sons. Things hadn't turned out the way he had planned.

I've dreamed of meeting them over the years and almost made it back to Tallahassee once or twice. There was never enough time or money. But when I discovered Liam was about to get married, I saved every penny for a bus ticket and a couple of weeks' motel stay. I want to attend the wedding and pick up where we left off many years ago.

But Liam made it clear he loves his Daisy and will do anything to keep from hurting her. Now I have to move on to Plan B. It won't be easy, but I will convince Liam and Donnie that their adoptive parents aren't the salt of the earth.

Curtis sat on the edge of the bed listening to the distant sound of children playing in the courtyard, a reminder of the years he'd miss with his boys. Sighing with disappointment, he rummaged through his tattered duffel bag. Curtis grabbed a small notebook, flipped through the pages until he came across a name and telephone number written in big bold print.

A slow smile crept across his face. Vera worked at the county office many years ago, and they dismissed her for misconduct. He'd chatted with her on and off over the years. And she was just the person he needed to contact.

He gripped the phone as if it held the key to his future. He tapped her number, and the line clicked. A few seconds later, she answered. "Hello?"

Her soft, sultry tone evoked all kinds of memories for Curtis. Vivid images of the two of them paraded across his mind. "Well, now, I'd know that voice anywhere. How are you doing, Vera? It's been too long."

"Curtis?" She did not sound pleased to hear from him. "What do you want? I told you not to call me again."

"Just checking on you. I'm in town. Thought we could hang out. You still over on Lafayette? You still baking those German chocolate cakes?"

"What do you want, Curtis?"

"A little of your time, that's all."

"That's what you always say. Tell me what you want, or I'm going to disconnect the call." Her words clipped with irritation.

"Remember back in the day when you worked for the county?"

"Yeah, so what?"

"So, you used to tell me how things weren't right over there. Papers got shuffled, files gone missing. That wasn't my imagination, was it?"

"No, it wasn't. I lost my job for talking too much. That should tell you enough."

"Exactly! You lost your job because of the system. And me, I lost my boys because of the system, too. They don't care about people like us."

"I didn't say all of that."

"You don't have to," said Curtis, growing annoyed and impatient. "You and I, we know the truth. Just a matter of putting two and two together."

"There's nothing we can do about it now. That was years ago. Just forget about it and move on. I did."

Curtis clenched his fist, struggling to keep his tone steady. "I tried, but I can't let it rest. People have been feeding my sons, who are now grown men, lies about me, first from their mother, then from the people who adopted them. It's time they heard the truth. You got a heart; I know you do. Don't you think they deserve to know the truth?"

"What they deserve is peace. Not you causing trouble."

"Peace comes from the truth, not from lies."

"There's nothing I can do for you, Curtis. My cousin works there now. I don't want trouble for me or her."

"Your cousin works for the county? Government work runs in the family, huh? What's her name again?"

"Connie. But she can't help you either, so don't you even try it."

"Connie? I remember her. Real pretty girl. Now don't you worry. She won't get in any trouble. Trust me."

"No, Curtis," barked Vera. "I'm not playing with you. Don't bring her into this."

"You can trust me." Curtis threw his head back with a nasty laugh. His chest swelled with hope. "I'll let you get back to whatever you were doing. Always a pleasure talking to you."

This is the break I needed. If Connie is anything like her cousin, she'll be easy to manipulate, especially if she's peeved with the system. It won't take much to convince her to help. Vera will forgive me later. She always does.

"Now all I need to do is figure out a way to get pretty girl Connie to help me rewrite history."

Chapter 14

The drive from Motel 6 to Donnie's place was tense. Liam gripped the steering wheel with his eyes locked forward. Donnie stared out the passenger window, his gaze sharp, and jaw tight. The anger was like a yard overtaken by invasive roots.

Liam punched the steering wheel. "You should've let me hit him. He deserved it."

"I stopped you because I didn't feel like posting bail tonight," said Liam, his foot bouncing.

"He has a lot of nerve accusing our parents of doing something illegal."

"He doesn't get to turn his back on us and begrudge the people who cared for us."

Liam continued to drive in silence, engulfed in a whirlwind of resentment. An unexpected phone call that led to a pointless encounter with his biological father had ruined his morning. A meeting that could change everything.

After dropping Donnie off at his place, Liam drove to the office and attempted to drown his thoughts in securing the permit for the tree removal project. Time was of the essence. If they didn't move quickly, the rain could delay the start of the project.

He worked uninterrupted until Daisy walked into his office.

"I'm getting ready to leave. Do you need my help with anything before I log off?" she asked with a wide smile.

"If you could put a rush on this tree removal project, that would be a tremendous help." He teased.

"What's the hold up?" She stared at him, her expression unreadable.

"I'm just kidding, Mom. There's nothing you can do. We've done our part. I'm waiting for approval from Growth Management."

"For the E & G Project?" Her eyes flashed with recollection.

"That's the one. I wish there were a way to cut through all the red tape."

Daisy's thoughtful eyes stared straight ahead, and he could tell she was processing information. "Sister Parks works there."

"Who?"

Daisy sighed, taking a seat across from him. "Thelia Parks. She's an usher at the church. You know her. Her son entered Howard last year."

Liam nodded. "Oh, yes. I know who you're referring to."

"I'll call her."

"What position does she have with Growth Management? Does she have any influence?"

She shrugged, rising from the chair. "I don't know. If she doesn't, perhaps, maybe she knows someone who does."

"Wouldn't hurt to try it."

"I'll be right back," she said, leaving the office.

Liam turned to the computer and began reviewing the steps to establish a safety zone around the tree. The team already identified power lines, fencing, and landscaping features. Once they granted the permit, the project would proceed at full speed. As the minutes wore on, he reviewed the timelines for several other upcoming projects.

Daisy returned.

Sister Park said that they had approved the permit. However, someone sent it to the wrong computer queue.

Liam elevated his hands in faux surrender. "You're kidding me? And they couldn't tell me that over the phone?"

"They probably didn't know where to look. Anyway, you will receive a confirmation email shortly."

"Thanks, Mom." Liam smiled. "I'm glad you had that connection."

"I've been around a long time, and I know many people. We all try to help each other."

He raised an eyebrow as his thoughts wandered. *Is that how you cut through the red tape of the adoption process?*

"If that's all you need, I'm going to leave. Zeke and I are going to get some Christmas shopping done."

"Sure, Mom. Thanks for your help."

"No problem. Remember, it's not always what you know. It's who you know." Daisy giggled and walked out the door.

Liam crumpled his brow, captivated by his mother's words. She had known to use a paradox from time to time, but there was something about her tone that captured his attention.

Chapter 15

Liam's promise to have dinner with Lorraine without discussing the promotion seemed like an impossible task. He didn't want to ask her to turn down an opportunity she'd not only worked hard to achieve, but one that may not come around again soon. But he didn't want to delay starting their family. Besides, she'd agreed to start a family right away.

Curtis and his threat to disrupt the wedding also battled for space in his mind. He'd come dangerously close to harming the man. Liam was grateful Donnie was there to intervene, but fearful that next time could be different. And he would end up in prison, repeating his biological father's behavior. He couldn't afford to let his rage toward Curtis obscure his judgment, not when he had so much to lose.

Liam walked through the glass doors of Shula's 347 Grille, ready to dine with his bride-to-be. The cascading canopy of hanging wine bottles above the dining room and the vibrant flatscreen TVs along the wall set the stage for a fun time. The atmosphere was a unique combination of casual and upscale for a lively date night. Having dinner with Lorraine was just what he needed.

He saw her sitting at a table near the window, and his heart pounded an erratic beat.

When Lorraine turned to see him, a warm smile appeared, and it nearly knocked him off his feet. He made his way over to the table and leaned in for a kiss.

Looking deep into her eyes, he muttered, "You look breathtaking."

"Thank you."

He settled in the chair across from her, eyes lingering, gentle, and sturdy.

"It sure smells good in here," he said, inhaling an assortment of grilled steaks and seafood.

Before Lorraine could reply, the server arrived. She greeted them with water and menus.

"Thank you," said Liam, and the server disappeared.

As he scanned the menu, his mother's words swirled through his mind. *Remember, it's not always what you know. It's who you know.*

He couldn't ignore the irony.

"You won't believe what happened at the office. An angry client came in and confronted one auditor. Can you imagine? Security had to escort him out ...," said Lorraine.

Liam muttered, "Uh-huh."

I won't sit idly by and let Curtis tarnish my parents' reputation ... but what if he's telling the truth?

"... Now they're talking about beefing up security for the building. I'm surprised they hadn't done it already. Clients become disgruntled for many reasons. Remember when they asked me to audit the books for Whittington Landscaping?" Lorraine continued.

Dad and Mom would do nothing illegal. Dad always taught us to follow the rules, to be aboveboard, to take the high road. But they wanted desperately to have children. And what were the chances of adopting two brothers?

"Are you listening?" asked Lorraine, her tone clipped.

Liam took a deep breath, forcing himself into the present. "I'm sorry. What were you saying?"

"What's on your mind?" she asked, appearing frustrated.

"Nothing. Why?"

Lorraine scoffed, her frustration clear. "Because you're giving me generic short answers. I know we agreed not to talk about the job offer until we get to the therapist's office. But if you're going to act like this, maybe we shouldn't spend time together until we meet with her."

As he struggled to answer, Liam wondered if he should tell Lorraine about his meeting with Curtis. It would be a relief to get it off his chest; however, he didn't want to upset her with Curtis' threats to stir up trouble at the wedding. But he recognized the anger and pain in her eyes. It hurt him to know he was the cause.

The waitress arrived to take their selections and disappeared again.

"I was thinking about Curtis. He called the office today."

"Oh, really," said Lorraine, raising an eyebrow. "What did he have to say?"

Liam gritted his teeth. "Bottom line is, he insisted on seeing me. He said he had something to tell me."

Lorraine clenched her jaw. "And he couldn't tell you over the phone?"

"He could have, but he insisted we meet. I grabbed Donnie, and we went over there together."

Lorraine listened intently as Liam relayed the story. Her lips parted in surprise. Liam included everything except the details about the wedding.

Her hand flew up automatically, but her shock lasted only a beat before she burst into laughter. "Give me a moment. I'm trying to wrap my head around this. You threw him against the wall?"

"I did."

"I'm sorry for laughing. I know violence is not the answer, but he deserved that."

"He should be grateful Donnie pulled me off of him."

The two of them sat silently at the table for a few seconds.

"What happened after that?"

"He accused my parents of obtaining Donnie and me through illegal means. Can you believe that?"

Lorraine's eyebrows flew to her hairline in surprise. "That's not what I expected you to say. Of course, I don't believe that. Your mom has shared your adoption story with me dozens of times. Because of limited availability and racial bias, they were on the waiting list for years."

Liam didn't respond. He just nodded his head in agreement.

"How's Donnie handling it?" She took a sip of water.

"He's furious. He said little on the ride home. I guess we were both too angry to talk about it. Donnie has always been curious about our birth parents. I didn't share his interest, but I'm glad he could get some answers. Probably not the ones he wanted."

"What's your next move? Are you going to tell your mother?"

"Absolutely not. I don't want to upset her?" Liam shook his head and pointed a finger in the air.

"Of course, she'll be upset, but …?

"Mom went into a deep depression after Dad died. It was difficult to watch, especially after I moved back into the house. She lost a lot of weight. We could barely get her to eat. All she wanted to do was sleep. Some days, we couldn't get her out of bed. Thank God for healing her. Now she has Zeke, and he seems to be good for her. She's smiling and laughing again."

"I'm so sorry you and your mother had to go through that. It's difficult to watch our parents suffer. But what if he contacts her?" Her eyelashes trembled under the weight of concern.

Liam shook his head in fury. "If he knows what's good for him, he won't."

"But what if he does, and she discovers that you and Donnie kept this from her?"

"I don't know. I guess we will have to deal with it then."

"If you're concerned about his accusations, let's do some digging. We'll get the information that proves him wrong. You don't know this man. He probably has an ulterior motive. I don't think he's just going to let it go."

Liam stared straight ahead and then threw his shoulders back in attention.

"I have some experience with this subject, remember?" said Lorraine, referring to the child she gave up for adoption when she was still in high school. "We can start there."

The waitress arrived with their dinner, giving Liam time to gather his thoughts.

What if Curtis isn't lying? No! Mom would never. I won't allow myself to think that.

The gravity of his uncertainty hung in the air like a thick cloud. He sensed it took Lorraine by surprise. He'd always doted on his mother, treating her like a queen.

"Do you believe his accusations?" asked Lorraine as soon as the server left.

"Dad and Mom were desperate to have children. People do strange things when they're desperate." Liam released a sharp exhale as if trying to blow the idea out of his head. "No! I don't believe Curtis."

Liam took a deep breath, forcing himself to calm down. He reached across the table for her hands and blessed the food.

Lorraine toyed with her salad. "I can do some digging around if you want me to."

Liam's mind raced. He didn't believe Curtis, but somewhere in the back of his mind, he wondered whether his parents had told them everything about the adoption. As much as he hated to admit it, Lorraine had a point. He needed proof before the wedding, which was only a few weeks away.

"That might take a lot of time; we have a wedding coming up."

"And we have a wedding planner who is keeping us on track. I want to do this for you, but I won't do it without your blessing. What do you say?"

Liam glanced across the table at the woman who would become his wife. She was beautiful, smart, and everything he wanted. She could have her choice of men. But she accepted his proposal. And now, even after he withheld his full support for her promotion, she will help him find information on his adoption. With a grateful heart, he thanked God for Lorraine.

Liam reached across the table for her hand. "Thank you, babe. You have my blessing."

Chapter 16

Thick gray clouds draped the Tallahassee sky like a warm winter blanket on Thursday morning. An unusually cold air mass covered the atmosphere. Most folks were unprepared for the sudden change, though meteorologists predicted the snap would last only a few days.

Lorraine tightened the jacket strap around her waist and darted to the sidewalk. Walking downtown usually felt like hopping onto a conveyor belt of Southern hospitality. Today, it was a shuffle of chilled salutations.

The promotion offer hung over her like frost on a fragile branch, one wrong move away from snapping. She could feel a chill in her chest. Lorraine steadied herself. They needed to discuss it, even if it changed everything about their wedding and the life they imagined.

Liam kept his word about not discussing the promotion during dinner the night before. But this morning, Kendra, the premarital counselor, planned to meet with them. Until now, the sessions had been about developing tools and knowledge to build a strong and lasting marriage. Today, they would discuss her promotion and how it could affect their marriage.

Within minutes, she arrived at the brick and glass building that housed Kendra Blake's practice. The open-air stairway led to a row of offices. Lorraine walked through the door, her eyes landing on a young couple in the lobby. The man held the woman's hand as they looked deep into each other's eyes with smiles. Lorraine hoped that she and

Liam would leave their appointment with the same look of love in their eyes.

"Good morning, Lorraine. Kendra will be out in just a moment," said the receptionist, glancing at the clock.

Lorraine turned to the cozy lounge beside the television. She picked up a *Psychology Today* magazine and pretended to read. Flipping through the pages, she could not focus.

Within seconds, the door reopened, and Liam appeared. Their eyes locked as if frozen in time.

"Hi, babe. Sorry, I'm late, had a hard time finding a place to park."

Before Lorraine could reply, Kendra entered the lobby from her office.

"Hey, guys. Come on back," she said with a welcoming smile.

They followed her through the door and down the small hallway. Once inside the office, Kendra gestured for the couple to have a seat on the couch.

"How's everything going?" asked Kendra, reaching for her iPad and Apple pencil. Then she slipped into the armchair.

Lorraine peered at the mixture of professional and uplifting books on the shelf, wondering how open and honest she should be. "It's been a tough week. There's something we can't seem to discuss without getting upset. So, we agreed to wait until this appointment to talk about it. We thought maybe you could help us."

"First things first." Kendra threw her shoulder back in attention. "I want to hear what our goals are for today. By the time the session is over, what do we want to walk away with and understand?"

Lorraine placed her hand over her heart. "I want Liam to understand what this promotion offer means to me."

"Is it your wish that you come away with some sort of agreement?" Kendra asked Lorraine. "Or is that not important for today?"

"Yes. That is important," said Lorraine with a curt nod.

"Is there anything else, without getting into the meat of it, in terms of goals for today?" Kendra tilted her head slightly.

"Liam, what about you? What do you want to walk out with?"

"I want us to be on the same page."

"Do I have permission to interrupt you both if we get off topic?" asked Kendra.

"Yes," said Lorraine.

Laim nodded his assent.

Kendra leaned forward. "Ok, who wants to tell me what's going on?"

Lorraine raised a finger and said, "I will. The company presented me with a promotion opportunity, the same one they denied me last year. I was so excited about the opportunity." She clenched her fist as she continued. "But when I told Liam, he wasn't as happy about it."

Kendra steepled her fingers. "That had to be difficult not to receive the promotion the first time around."

Lorraine recalled hearing that she had not received the promotion. She felt as if something had knocked the breath out of her. It didn't feel like a decision. It felt like a betrayal.

"Yes, it was." The furrow in Lorraine's eyebrows deepened. "And now that they have offered it to me again, I'm not sure what to do."

"So, right now, how are you feeling about not knowing what you're going to do?" asked Kendra.

"I'm afraid because our wedding is just a few weeks away," said Lorraine, throwing her hands in the air.

"What are the emotions you feel when you think about the fact that there's no answer or a plan at this point?"

Lorraine swallowed hard. "I'm scared, and I'm sad."

"Is there anything else you'd like to add to that before we turn it over to Liam?"

"No," said Lorraine, slowly shaking her head.

Kendra leaned toward Liam. "Tell me what's going on in your understanding."

Liam sat erect, glanced at Lorraine, and then turned to Kendra. "Well, when we decided to get married, we agreed on a plan to start a family right away."

Lorraine shook her head, unable to meet his eyes. She hated disappointing him. Her heart felt heavier than ever, especially since she knew how much Liam wanted to be a father.

"Tell me about that look on your face, Lorraine," said Kendra.

"We all make plans. But plans change and things happen."

Kendra made a note on her iPad before continuing. "So is the issue the timeline, or is one of you concerned that starting a family is not the plan anymore?"

"The plan is more of a permanent agreement that we put in place. My concern is if the offer is going to change our plan, what else is going to change our plan?" asked Liam, crossing his arms.

Kendra turned to Lorraine. "Do you understand what Liam is saying?"

"Yes. I suppose I do." Lorraine rolled her eyes again.

"Tell me what's on your mind. What's the eye rolling about?" asked Kendra.

"First, I haven't decided about the job," said Lorraine, her words sharp and cutting. "I haven't accepted the position."

"That's an excellent point," said Kendra. "Liam, were you under the impression that she had already decided about this?"

"Yes, I was. That's why we're here."

"So, can we put that piece to rest?" Kendra pressed her palms together firmly. "Because it seems like that was a myth coming in. Now we're all on the same page."

Lorraine turned to Liam. "I'm glad you understand that."

"Ok, but there's still an element there," said Kendra, shaking a finger in the air. "Even though no one has decided. Liam, let me ask you, is there any other emotion you can describe that makes it even a question whether she is going to take the job? Are you even a little upset that she is even thinking about this?"

Liam looked at the bookcase as if it held the answer. After a moment of contemplation, he said, "I'm guarded and prepared for the worst-case scenario. My anxiety stems from the fact that Lorraine is even debating her decision. This could go either way. Her not accepting it doesn't mean she won't accept it. It's an unresolved issue that will impact the rest of our lives. Our wedding is in two weeks," said Liam, his words abrupt and short.

"We don't even know how long it will take me to get pregnant," replied Lorraine. "It might take months. It might take years. I can accept the position and work until I get pregnant and have the baby."

"What if you get pregnant right away? Then what?" countered Liam.

Lorraine drummed her fingers on the arm of the couch, knowing this moment could change everything.

"That's true," she said, imagining his words unfolding.

Liam appeared frustrated. "So, what are you going to do?"

"But what if we plan to start our family in about a year. That way, I can accept the position. Then, when I get pregnant, I'll take a leave of absence." She offered with imposed assurance. But her heart teemed with uncertainty.

"I hear you," he said, casting a faraway stare. "But because you failed on our initial agreement, I don't have a lot of confidence that you will follow through."

"So, Liam, are you saying that the plan Lorraine proposed, you don't believe her?" asked Kendra, palms up and open. "Are you saying that you don't believe the words that are coming out of her mouth because when the time comes around, she might change her mind again?"

Liam pressed his lips together again. "Yes."

Silence fell over the room.

Shattered, Lorraine placed her hand over her mouth. She felt as if the ground had given way.

Kendra turned to Lorraine. "Think about that. I want you to honestly think about it because in Liam's mind, that's what's happening now. You had a plan with Liam, and you might change them. You make another plan, and you might change that one. Liam doesn't believe the words that are coming out of your mouth."

Lorraine lowered her head and blinked back tears as shock turned into shame and disappointment.

He doesn't believe me. Lord, help … Liam really doesn't believe me. If he doesn't trust me now, what happens after the marriage?

"I want you both to think about that." Kendra softened her tone. "Let's entertain the idea that plans change. And they will change because you guys are not machines, you are people. But it is important that you can take each other's words at face value."

Lorraine and Liam exchanged wounded glances.

"Lorraine, how do you feel about the fact that you tried to offer a plan that Liam might think was a good idea, but he also doesn't believe you will commit to that plan. What do you think about that?"

"It makes me sad because I haven't shown him that I won't keep my word, but I guess I have," admitted Lorraine, tucking her chin to her chest.

Liam turned to Lorraine. "I know I sound harsh, but my concern is, will your career always be the headliner?"

"Ok. Now we have new information," said Kendra, finger pointing upward. "Lorraine, I wonder if it would be helpful because sometimes you must go back and double down and reassure. When you presented your new plan, did you really mean, let's start a year from now, no matter what happens? Is that what you really meant to say or to commit to?"

Lorraine pressed her fingers together. "Yes, I want a family. I really do. I also want to take this opportunity at work. But it's not more important to me than family. If I were to get pregnant right away, of course, I would choose our family. I'm just saying, let's delay starting the family for a year."

"And before Liam responds, we have more information in here, so it seems like we're operating under a new system." Kendra drew an invisible line in the air. "You say that if you were to get pregnant right away, you would prioritize the family. I think that is new information to Liam. I think he had rolled all the prior information in his mind, and we must dispel what is not true. Is that the case, Liam?"

"Yes."

"So, something like this is going to happen again," said Kendra, drawing a circular motion with her hand. "But let's zoom out. It's okay to plan because that is how you operate. We plan the best we can because that provides security, comfort, and reassurance. But you both are human beings. It's not about one of you; it's about how you function together. Plans are like an outline, so we know that we can expect changes. Make sure you're on the same page. Before, you just had to make sure you knew what page you were on. Now you have to know what page you are on collectively in terms of what you're going to prioritize and then move from there."

Lorraine slowly moved her eyes to meet Liam's. They held each other's gaze. Suddenly, it was as if they were the only ones in the room. Liam reached for her hand. A tender smile found its place, and an unspoken peace fell upon her.

"The test of uncertainty was great. This will happen again. This is about the process you're going to go through when you're dealing with uncertainty. When this happens, think about the assumptions, narratives, and experiences that you have. Just because it's an assumption doesn't mean you're wrong or right. Just identify that it is an assumption. You're both equipped to deal with that, and if you have difficulty, you can come here. It sounds like you both have lots of support from both of your families. You have a support network. I commend you both. Is there anything else?"

"No. Thank you so much for helping us work through this."

Lorraine laced her fingers through Liam's, their hands trembling yet reassuring. A tear slipped free, but it wasn't from hurt; it was from relief. She whispered, "Thank you, Jesus." She met Liam's eyes and saw promise. It wasn't a promise that everything would be easy. It was reassurance that, whatever came next, they would face it together.

Chapter 17

Thursday morning, Lorraine stood in the Crystal Ballroom at the Elegant Events Center, thanking God that Liam and she had reached an amicable agreement. Now they could fully concentrate on their fast-approaching wedding date. Bri's authoritative voice interrupted her thoughts.

"You'll have two hours to set up before the reception begins and one hour to clean up after the event." Bri tapped her Apple watch several times in a gesture to the caterer.

Liam, Lorraine, Daisy, and Zeke were meeting with the vendors hired for the soiree. The Crystal Ballroom showcased sophisticated chandeliers, elegant window coverings, and mirrored panels. The couple chose that location because it had hosted their engagement party, which was special to them. Bri explained to everyone the expectations for the wedding reception.

"Remember, tasks that take five minutes to complete on a normal day will take thirty minutes on the wedding day," said Bri, conducting the final walk-through like a well-trained maestro.

"She knows her stuff," Daisy whispered to Lorraine.

Lorraine nodded. "And she loves what she does. I don't know how I would have managed without her."

"The DJ's booth and speakers will be here," Bri pointed to the stage. "Cake and dessert table ..."

Bri's words faded to the background as Lorraine looked at Liam. His body was in the building with the rest of them, but she could tell by his facial expression that his mind was someplace else. He was probably thinking about Curtis and his outrageous accusations.

I hate to see him so uptight. Maybe I'll pick Daisy's brains about the adoption. Curtis Barnes is up to something, and I'm going to find out what it is. His claims about the adoption are a lie, and I plan to prove it. But first, I need the name of the lawyer who handled everything. Daisy has that information. But how do I get her to tell me without arousing her suspicions?

"Lorraine?" Bri's voice broke through her musing.

"Huh?" She turned to see everyone looking at her. What had she missed?

"Is there something you'd like to add?" asked Bri.

"No. You've thought of everything."

"Glad to hear it. That's my job. If you think of anything between now and the wedding, shoot me a text or a call. Otherwise, that's all I have. You all can go now."

Bri gathered her things, and within minutes, she and the vendors were out the door.

"Now that's a shrewd businesswoman," said Liam. "She promised to have us in and out of here in less than an hour, and she did it."

"We all know that time is money." Daisy's tone was sincere as she waved a hand in the air.

"Don't I know it." Zeke reached over and squeezed Daisy's hand. "I'd take you to lunch, but I have another meeting in about twenty minutes."

"I understand," said Daisy.

Liam crossed the room and offered Zeke a handshake. "Thank you again for allowing us to use your facility for the reception. It's perfect."

"My pleasure, young man," said Zeke. "Besides, it allows me to rack up brownie points with your mother."

"I don't think you have to worry much about that." Liam leaned back, smiling. "Just keep treating her right, and you'll be fine."

"You have my word," said Zeke, placing a soft kiss on Daisy's forehead, waving to Lorraine, and retreating out the door.

"I need to leave, too." Liam pulled his mother in for a bear hug. Then he turned to Lorraine and brushed a kiss across her lips. "I'll call you later."

"Okay." Lorraine smiled and watched him walk away.

"I guess that leaves you and me," said Daisy, strapping her purse across her shoulder. "Would you like to join me for lunch, or do you have a meeting as well?"

After contemplating the possibilities for a moment, Lorraine spoke with enthusiasm, "I'd love to."

"How about we meet at Ma's Diner in thirty minutes?"

"I'll be there." Lorraine reached for her purse, satisfied with the progress of the wedding plans and overjoyed with the opportunity to have lunch with Daisy. Maybe this was the break she was looking for.

***

Minutes later, Lorraine stepped into Ma's Diner, a local eatery known for its down-home meals and Southern hospitality. A buttery haze of grilled onions and seasoned beef wafted throughout the area. Lunchtime patrons filled most of the tables, booths, and counter seating. She scanned the charming cafe and found no sign of Daisy.

"How many in your party, honey?" asked the server, with a notepad in one hand, the other hand on her hip, and a pen tucked behind her ear.

Lorraine smiled. "Two. She'll be here shortly."

"Ok. Let's get you seated, and I'll take your drink order."

Lorraine followed the woman to a cozy booth near the back of the restaurant. She ordered water for herself and ordered sweet tea for Daisy. She admired many things about her soon-to-be mother-in-law, especially how she balanced work and family. That's why she felt a little uneasy about the sneaky way she planned to glean information without her knowledge.

Daisy entered the door and hurried toward her. She slid into the booth across from Lorraine.

"Have you been waiting long?" she asked, casting a curious smile.

"No, not at all."

After a few moments, the server returned. They ordered BLTs and split an order of fries.

"How are your parents doing?" asked Daisy.

"They're fine," Lorraine replied, brushing a strand of hair from her face. "Dad's at a medical convention in Chicago. Mom keeps busy with church activities and helping me with wedding plans."

Daisy took a sip of her tea and swallowed. "We're all excited for you and Liam. You know, Liam never dated a lot. Always talked about holding out for the right one. I believe you are the right one."

"Thank you. I'm blessed to have him. I'm excited. Didn't realize how much work planning a wedding would be." Lorraine glanced behind the counter at the antique turntable and various record albums.

"I know the wedding day is special, but you two will have a lifetime together. I'm proud of both of you. How are things going with the house?"

"Everything is going as planned."

"Liam shared some of his landscaping ideas with me. He reminds me of Harold. He worked hard to turn the backyard into a beautiful oasis. Then he turned it into a playground when the boys came along. I'm sure Liam will do the same."

The server returned with their order, and Lorraine gathered her thoughts. After Daisy blessed the food, Lorraine bit into her sandwich, taking a moment to enjoy the savory bacon.

Asking too many questions could lead to false assumptions. So, Lorraine took her time setting the stage for gathering bits and pieces of information along the way.

"Yes. We're looking forward to the day when we'll have children running around the backyard. We're already talking about it," said Lorraine. "Did you and Mr. Whittington always plan to have children?"

"We did. Of course, we wanted to have them the traditional way. But that wasn't God's plan for us. So, we adopted."

"I love the story you tell about when you first met Liam and Donnie. You seem to remember everything, even what they were wearing."

Daisy looked in the distance as if it held an image. "Oh, I'll never forget. It was a special day."

"Who handled the adoption for you? Do you remember the attorney's name?" Lorraine poked a French fry with her fork, dipped it in the blob of ketchup, and took a small bite.

Daisy crinkled her brow. "Are you and Liam thinking of adopting?"

"No ma'am. I was just curious. I apologize if I overstepped."

"No, you didn't," said Daisy, waving a dismissive hand in the air. "Our attorney was Jeremiah Jones. He had an office downtown. We used to keep in touch with him, but we lost contact. Good-looking black man. But don't tell Zeke I said that." Teased Daisy. "Let's talk about the honeymoon. Are you excited?"

Lorraine made a mental note of the attorney's name before answering. "Yes! An entire week without deadlines, e-mails, and spreadsheets! Plus, it will be my first time visiting Jamaica."

As they continued chatting, Lorraine couldn't help but think about Attorney Jeremiah Jones. Daisy seemed comfortable sharing his name. Surely, she would not have shared the information so easily if she had been trying to hide something?

Even though she got what she needed, the weight of what she now knew sat heavily on Lorraine's heart. Could the attorney lead them to the truth? Would the truth counter Curtis' lies? Would Liam receive the clarity he longed for? She would do everything in her power to help him, no matter what it cost.

***

Liam sat alone in his office later that afternoon, reviewing specs for an upcoming project. His phone vibrated, interrupting his thoughts.

"Hello."

"The lawyer's name is Jeremiah Jones." Lorraine's excitement pierced through the phone.

There was a pause on the line as Liam traced the name from his childhood. "That's right. Dad and Mom used to talk about him all the time. Thanks, babe."

"You're welcome. What's your next move?"

Liam felt a twinge of apprehension. "First, I'm going to find out what I can about Attorney Jones. Then I'll determine the next move based on what I discover."

"Great. I'm pulling into the parking lot at work. Wanted to give you that information before heading in. Let me know if you need me to do anything else."

"I will. Were you pleased with the way things went at the walk-through this morning?"

"Yes."

Liam could almost see her smiling through the phone. That pleased him.

"Were you?" she asked.

"I was. Still can't believe we'll be married soon. And you'll be Mrs. Lorraine Whittington, for always and forever."

"I like the sound of that," said Lorraine, her voice filled with expectation.

They chatted for a few minutes longer before concluding the call.

Liam stared at the name written on the sticky note in front of him. He sat still for a moment, pondering the next move. He typed The Florida Bar into the computer search bar, then paused. His eyes scanned the screen as it loaded slowly. Then he entered the name: Jeremiah Jones.

Let's find out a little about you, Mr. Jones. What's your reputation as a lawyer? Do you have a habit of practicing shady law?

The name pulled up quickly, bringing with it a list of credentials, dates, and quiet questions. The truth waited in hyperlinks and fine print.

He read aloud, "You've been practicing since 1983 ... Attended FAMU College of Law ...and no disciplinary record for the past ten years. You're a board-certified adoption lawyer. Why am I not surprised? Of course, Dad would want only the best lawyer."

Liam leaned back in his chair, crossing one leg over the other, measuring what he knew against what he needed to find out. He grabbed the phone and dialed his brother's number.

"What's up, bro?" answered Donnie.

"Got a name and a number for the adoption lawyer. What do you say we make an appointment to see Mr. Jeremiah Jones?"

"He's still practicing?" asked Donnie, surprise in his voice.

"Yes. Downtown."

"How are we going to get an appointment? Do you think he'll see us, given the attorney-client privilege rules?"

Donnie made a good point. Liam considered a few options before suggesting, "What if Lorraine and I scheduled a meeting to talk to him about adoption? No need to be specific. We'll get into the details once we're in his office. It's not a lie, that is the reason we want to talk with him."

"I'm fine with that."

Liam's eyebrows rose. "I'm sure Lorraine will be eager to help."

"I'm sure she will. She'll do anything for you, bro."

Liam disconnected the call and thought about his brother's words. It wouldn't be difficult to convince Lorraine to go along with the idea. She wanted to prove Curtis wrong as much as Liam and Donnie did.

Chapter 18

The following Thursday morning, Liam drove into Lorraine's condo parking lot with a grin tugging at his face. He jumped out, rounded the car with purpose, and flung the passenger door open like he was late for their first date.

"Thank you, kindly," she murmured, smiling as he reached for her hand.

Before she could slide into the seat, he cupped her face and kissed her. Then he nodded toward the car. "Let's go."

"Thanks for coming to get me. I really didn't want to drive separate cars." Lorraine broke into a wide smile. "Is Donnie going to meet us afterward? Or are you going to call him?"

"I'm going to call him. We'll see each other," said Liam.

He closed the passenger door, walked around the vehicle, and slipped into the driver's seat. He started the engine and drove out of the parking lot.

"I did some more research on Jeremiah. It seems he's quite involved in the community," said Liam.

"What do you mean?" Lorraine glanced pointedly in Liam's direction.

"He offers a free informational session at the community center."

"And?" Again, Lorraine cast Liam an inquisitive glance.

"He answers questions about adoption, foster care, guardianship, and family reunification," he said. "It seems he's invested in the idea of family."

"Oh, that's intriguing." Perhaps we saw him and weren't aware of his identity, Lorraine offered.

"It's possible."

As he traveled down the busy thoroughfare, Liam felt a sense of peace about meeting Jeremiah Jones. He recalled hearing his mother say how worried she was about the process when they were adopting and how comfortable she was working with him. That had to count for something. If the attorney had understood the severity of the situation, maybe he would have been more forthcoming with the information.

Liam and Lorraine pulled into an open spot in one of the downtown parking garages. Liam took a deep breath as he mentally prepared for the meeting. He held Lorraine's hand as they walked the two blocks to the attorney's office. He imagined his father and mother taking the same steps many years ago. Were they nervous? Were they hopeful?

Lorraine was quieter than he'd seen her in a long time. Perhaps she could feel Liam's anxiety. She stopped mid-stride and looked into his eyes. "Are you ready?" she lovingly asked.

"Ready as I'll ever be," said Liam, although resentment grew like weeds in the middle of his heart. This should not be happening. He should not be in the middle of downtown Tallahassee preparing to meet the attorney who handled the adoption for his parents. He was supposed to be working and planning a future with his fiancée.

Together, they walked up the path leading to the historic home, repurposed for business. Liam opened the door and stepped aside, allowing Lorraine to enter first.

A young blonde, in her twenties, looked away from her computer to greet them. "Hello. May I help you?"

"I'm Liam Whittington, and this is my fiancée, Lorraine Davis. We have an appointment with Attorney Jones."

"Of course." She glanced at her computer screen before turning back to them. "He'll be right out. Would you like something to drink while you wait?"

"No. Thank you," answered Liam before turning to Lorraine, who also declined.

"You're welcome to have a seat anywhere you like. If you change your mind about the beverages, our coffee station is to the left."

Liam steered Lorraine toward the small settee across from the wooden cart that housed water, coffee, and tea.

"Is this okay?" he asked.

"Sure." She slid onto the settee.

Liam positioned himself next to her, admiring the gallery wall of family-oriented quotes and framed Tallahassee landmarks. He shut his eyes and tilted his head back. Memories suddenly transported him back into childhood. He played football in the backyard with his dad and Donnie. His parents cheered from the sidelines when he beat the buzzer with the winning shot at a high school game—a guided trip through the Grand Canyon during a family vacation. The birthday celebrations made him feel like the most important kid on the planet.

After a few moments, a round-faced, bald gentleman entered. He wore a smile that gave the impression he was genuinely glad to see them.

"Good morning, Mr. Whittington, Miss Davis. I'm Jeremiah Jones. It's nice to meet you."

Liam stood, and they exchanged handshakes.

"Thank you for taking the time to meet with us, Attorney Jones. This is my fiancé, Lorraine."

"Call me Jeremiah. It's a pleasure to meet both of you. Please, follow me to my office."

The couple ambled back to Jeremiah's office. An assortment of file folders and paperwork covered the large oak desk, leaving only a small cleared space directly in front of his chair. He motioned to the pair of winged-back chairs facing the desk. "Have a seat, and tell me how I can help?"

"You handled the adoption process for my parents, Harold and Daisy Whittington," said Liam. He studied the attorney's face, looking for a glimmer of recognition of his parents' names.

Jeremiah leaned back in his chair and crossed his arms in front of his chest, saying nothing.

"I have a few questions about the adoption," Liam continued.

"Let me stop you," he said, waving a gentle hand in the air. "Florida seals adoption records." That includes birth certificates. A court order is the only way to open them. The only thing I can help you with is the birth parents' names."

"I understand. I have the names of my birth parents," said Liam, a twinge of exasperation creeping into his voice. "My sperm donor is the reason I'm here."

Unmoved by the sarcasm, Jeremiah rested his elbows on the arms of his chair and steepled his fingers. "Is your birth father not willing to answer your questions?"

"No, he's not," Liam sighed, shaking his head. "Let me explain. I recently heard from him for the first time in my entire life. The only thing he's willing to do is to make accusations about an illegal adoption."

"That's a serious allegation." Jeremiah leaned forward in his chair. "I invite you to contact the Florida Bar."

"I'm not accusing you of doing anything illegal," Liam let his words sink in. "We contacted the Florida Bar, and your record is impeccable."

Everyone has the right to their own opinion. However, facts are another matter. "What about your birth mother?"

"She's deceased."

"How about your adoptive parents. Are they willing to help?" asked Jeremiah, his eyes flickering with concern.

"My father is deceased, and I don't want to bring this to my mother." Liam slightly tilted his head. "The whole thing could be very upsetting for her."

Jeremiah pinched the bridge of his nose. "I understand you don't want to upset her. But she could provide first-hand information about the adoption."

Liam rubbed his hands across his eyes. "Absolutely not," Liam said, fortitude clear in his voice.

"Then, I recommend you petition the Clerk of the Court to unseal the records and investigate. Unfortunately, that is about all that I can do."

Liam dropped his head.

Lorraine shifted in her seat, appearing to be uneasy. "How long does that process usually take?"

Jeremiah mentioned that they typically completed the investigations within sixty days unless any unforeseen circumstances came up.

Lorraine glanced at Liam as if she were concerned about his reaction.

"Great. I don't have sixty days," Liam stated cynically.

"I wish I could help you. However, I cannot assist you."

"We understand," Lorraine offered, perhaps attempting to defuse the tension.

Liam thanked him for his time and stood up.

Jeremiah walked around to the front of the desk and extended his hand out to Liam. They shook hands.

Lorraine thanked him again, and they left the building

"Don't be angry with him," Lorraine said with tenderness. "He's not willingly withholding information. The law binds him."

Liam offered a hint of a smile, even though his mind was still processing the attorney's words. "I know. But it frustrates me so much when all he has to do is search his records and confirm everything was done by the books."

Lorraine sighed. She wrapped her hand around his waist. They embraced for a moment, then Liam pulled away. "Guess I should get you to your car so you can head to work."

Downtown Tallahassee flew by the window in rapid glimmers, along with Leon High School, blinking traffic lights, and a woman waiting at a crosswalk with a dog that looked just as tired as she did. Each scene came into focus just long enough to be spotted, then disappeared, engulfed by the next—even the live oaks blurred by like shadows.

Liam really wasn't watching, though. His eyes were in the city, but his mind was somewhere else. Her mind snagged on the reflection of the meeting with Jeremiah.

"What are you going to do now?" asked Lorraine, breaking the silence.

His heart plummeted at her inquiry. He gave her a small smile, hoping it conveyed the confidence he wished he possessed.

"I'm not sure. Guess I'll have to take one seed at a time."

"One seed at a time," Lorraine agreed, stroking his hand with encouragement.

***

With Lorraine safely in her car, Liam headed to Donnie's place.

Jeremiah Jones offered little information, so perhaps Donnie could suggest what they should do next.

Curtis wanted an invitation to the wedding. That would not happen. But what if Curtis showed up uninvited? What if he broadcast his malicious lies publicly to anyone who listened? If true, the ranting would humiliate his mother. Curtis could easily turn Lorraine's dream wedding into a nightmare. They would never forgive him. Or so he thought. All his worries were tied to Curtis Barnes. The man was bad news, and Liam wished he'd never come back into their lives.

He slowed to a stop in front of Donnie's place and shut off the engine. His anger intensified with every step toward the front door. Out of nowhere, he had a flashback from childhood. It happened one summer during Vacation Bible School. The children had to memorize a Scripture. On the last day, each of them had to quote their memory verse in front of the entire congregation. After they assigned it to him, he practiced saying his verse in the mirror every day. When it was his turn to recite his verse, Liam stood tall, and with confidence he quoted, "And be ye kind one to another, tenderhearted, forgiving one another, even as God for Christ's sake hath forgiven you. Ephesians chapter four, verse thirty-two."

Pausing halfway to the entrance, Liam realized he wasn't being Christlike. God required him to forgive. Still, he didn't see how that would be possible. Not only had this Curtis abandoned them as children, but he dared to reenter their lives with demands and cause havoc. He placed forgiving Curtis in the back of his mind and approached the front door. He rang the doorbell.

Donnie answered immediately. "I thought you were going to call. How did it go?"

"Not good."

"Really?" Donnie peeped over Liam's shoulder. "Is Lorraine with you?"

"No," said Liam. Then he followed Donnie to the living room and began pacing the floor.

"What happened at the attorney's office?" asked Donnie, leaning against a wall.

"He didn't offer any new information."

"Did he at least confirm that the adoption was on the up-and-up?"

Liam glanced at the framed photo of their parents on the console. Their beaming faces smiled into the camera. "No. He didn't deny it either. He suggested we contact The Florida Bar, which I'd already done. Jeremiah Jones' record is clean. I suppose he thinks that should be enough to put our minds at ease."

Donnie placed his hands across his chest. "I agree with him."

"Well, I don't." Liam stopped in place and turned to Donnie with his hands knotted into fists at his side.

"I think we should trust him. And we should trust Mom and Dad."

"Hmm."

"Even when we were kids, I was the one who wanted to know about our birth parents." Donnie pointed to his chest. "Not that I didn't trust Mom and Dad, I just wanted to know more about where I came from. You never wanted to talk about it, and you never wanted to know more. Why weren't you curious?"

Holding his hands up, Liam asked, "What else did I need to know? Mom and Dad were great parents. They worked hard to provide for us. They loved us. That was all I needed to know."

He stared at Donnie for a moment, as though there was more he wanted to say.

"Why was that enough?" Donnie arched his brow in question.

"What?"

"Was it because you thought you'd learn our birth parents were awful people, and they never loved us? Or were you worried that if you ever met them, you would have to forgive them?"

Donnie's words immediately set Liam on edge. Was unforgiveness written on his face? Guilt-stricken, Liam looked down at his clenched fist. "Don't be ridiculous."

"Okay, then what was it? Were you concerned that something was wrong with the way they adopted us?" Donnie frowned at his brother with accusation in his eyes.

"No." Liam clamped his fist so tight his hand ached.

"Then why are you concerned about whether the adoption was legal? If Curtis is lying, who cares what he says? Either you trust Dad and Mom or you don't."

A knot of tension tightened in Liam's chest. He knew Donnie had a point. But the battle with Curtis was far from over. "I came here to let you know what happened during the meeting with the attorney. Now you know. I'm going back to work now."

Liam didn't wait for a reply. The door slammed behind him, and the air outside hit like a hard slap.

Chapter 19

Friday morning, Lorraine made her way down the busy halls of Hamilton and Dunn. She caught sight of Steve Holloway through his open office door, with his focus on the computer screen in front of him.

She planned on informing him of her decision to accept the position.

Breathing in, she looked into the office. "Mr. Holloway?"

He turned to face her, his gaze frosted and piercing.

Lorraine paused mid-step. "I apologize. I can tell you're busy."

"I need your findings from the Baked to Perfection audit before the end of the day," he said, returning his attention to the computer screen.

"No problem. I'll get it to you as soon as possible."

"Yes. Thanks," he grumbled.

Lorraine had learned not to let much of his tone bother her. Mr. Holloway had few people skills, but he was a top-notch auditor. Most of the time, his tone and demeanor were ambiguous.

She obliged his request and retreated to her cubicle.

Lorraine spent the rest of the morning returning emails. Then, she uploaded the data to complete the Baked to Perfection report. She'd completed the fieldwork, which included gathering financial data. Her job was to complete the report based on the evidence found.

Baked to Perfection maintains excellent records. It certainly makes my job easier. Wonder why more businesses don't take the time to maintain and verify source documents. That simple step would save the company and the auditor a lot of time.

I suppose it's neglecting to verify source documents that keeps auditors like me in business. Source documents …

The implication of those two words triggered a landmine of thoughts.

Attorney Jones said that Florida adoption records were sealed. He advised us to petition the clerk of the court. If source documents are crucial for verifying financial transactions, they're also crucial for verifying adoption transactions. It's possible the closed documents are unavailable to me; perhaps something helpful can be located there.

Lorraine completed the report and sent it via email to Mr. Holloway, accompanied by a message stating her intention to have a lengthy lunch.

***

Instead of stopping for a meal during her lunch hour, Lorraine headed downtown to the clerk of the courts' office.

The receptionist sat behind the counter with her eyes focused on the computer screen.

Lorraine steeled herself. She did not know what was coming. Although the records were sealed, she hoped her questions wouldn't arouse undue suspicion. At the very least, she hoped to gain some new information from her visit.

"Good afternoon," said Lorraine, maintaining a cool and balanced demeanor.

The middle-aged clerk looked up from her computer. "Hello."

Lorraine read the clerk's name tag aloud. "Meg, I'd like to request access to an adoption record."

Meg's eyes tightened with conviction. "Statue seals adoption records. Are you the adoptee or attorney of record?"

"No, I'm not. The adoptee is my fiancé."

"Is he here?"

"No, but …"

Meg crossed her arms, then uncrossed them. "I could release it to him, but only if he had a court order or a signed, notarized authorization. I can't release it to you or even show you the file."

Lorraine leaned on the counter. "Are you able to see when the file was last viewed? Or updated? Just curious."

"Are you requesting information about the last time someone viewed it?" asked Meg. Her tone was professional but snappy. "Case number?"

"I don't have a case number, although I have the names of the birth and adoptive parents."

Meg glanced over her shoulder before accepting the document. She sat stiffly behind her desk, fingers hovering over the keyboard.

Watching Meg's body language, a tidal wave of thoughts and emotions flooded Lorraine's mind. She appreciated the woman's help but didn't want to get her into trouble. Suddenly, she became hyperaware of every sound. A computer hummed nearby, footsteps clacked in the hallway, and an office phone rang in the distance.

"Hmm, that's strange." Meg paused, raised an eyebrow, and studied the screen.

Lorraine leaned in. "What is it?"

"Someone accessed the file a week ago."

"Is that odd?"

"No. Not usually. It's just that it was sitting with no movement for so long. Then, in a week, several inquiries presented themselves."

"Several? Can you tell me who accessed the record?" asked Lorraine, a slight inflection in her voice.

"And why do you need to find that out?"

"Just curious."

Meg said, "I can't tell you who it was because the name is not listed," pausing for a second as if in deep thought. She tapped the keyboard, and the printer whirred.

"Oh, wow! Shouldn't a name and ID be required to access the record?" Lorraine tapped a finger against the countertop.

"You're right; they are. I can't explain what happened here. I am required to report this."

"Are you sure about that? I don't want to get you into trouble."

"Don't worry about me. It's my job to catch inconsistencies."

"It's a big request, but could you tell me your discoveries?"

Meg pulled a document from the printer and placed it in a manila folder. "I'm not sure I can do that …"

She recognized that Meg's reluctance was because of the checks and balances put in place to protect innocent parties.

"It's fine. You've already helped more than you know."

Meg's expression softened, but Lorraine could tell she was still concerned.

Lorraine took a deep breath. She didn't have the file, but she had something just as important — proof that someone accessed the files without proper identification. And she believed she knew exactly who it was.

***

The midafternoon sun trickled through the blinds of Liam's office. A prospective landscaping design plan was displayed on his computer screen. He reviewed it and considered whether he could execute it within the client's budget. Perhaps a discussion with the client was in order. He needed to determine which elements were most important and adjust the project accordingly.

It's difficult, but it can be done. Thank God for software that allows precise measurement and realistic renderings. I wonder how Dad expanded the company so fast without current technology. He and Mom were a power couple.

He sat back in the chair, tapping his fingers on the desk. His thoughts wandered to a more private matter. Liam pondered his and his brother's futures absent their adoptive parents' choice. What if they were separated? Would they have moved from foster home to foster home? Would they have become victims of abuse? He would never know because Harold and Daisy Whittington chose them and gave them a life they never could have dreamed of.

The vibrating phone interrupted his musing. He saw Lorraine's face on the screen, and his body stiffened. She probably wanted to discuss the meeting with Jeremiah. He took a deep breath, preparing himself for the conversation.

"Hey, baby. What's up?" he answered.

"I discovered something interesting," she said, her voice hurried.

He sat up in his chair. "What's that?"

"You know how I talk about checking source documents for my clients?"

Liam felt a hint of annoyance. "Yes, I do. If you're about to give me an auditing lesson, I promise you we're saving every receipt that comes through Whittington Landscaping. We've learned our lesson."

"That's good to know, but that's not what I was talking about," she said. "I was thinking about the source documents for your adoption. They're housed at the clerk's office."

"Yes. Jeremiah told us they had sealed them."

"Yes, he did. But I wanted to see for myself."

Liam's heart raced. "What did you do, Lorraine?"

"I took a chance and visited the Leon County Clerk of Courts."

Liam wanted to be angry. He wanted to tell Lorraine to leave well enough alone. But curiosity got the best of him. "Did you gain access to the records?"

"No, I didn't. But guess what I learned?"

"What's that?" Liam frowned.

Lorraine recapped her lunchtime excursion.

"It must have been Curtis. I had a feeling he was up to something. There's more to this story than meets the eye," said Lorraine.

Liam froze. Curtis' voice gnawed at the back of his mind. *What if it wasn't Curtis?* The thought struck fast, like a sucker punch, and he clenched his fists until his nails bit into his palms. *No, Mom never would.* He ran his hand over his face. *Don't even go there.*

Liam shook his head and released a sigh. "It had to be Curtis."

"What are you going to do?"

"I don't know," said Liam, irritation in his voice.

He gazed into the distance. His brows furrowed as he rubbed the back of his neck. "I don't think you understand. You have a perfect family. You have had your birth parents your entire life."

"You, above anyone else, are aware my family has flaws. Did you forget I had to surrender a child for adoption?"

"No. I haven't forgotten," said Liam, troubled by her argumentative tone. "But it's not the same. You're comparing apples to oranges."

An uncomfortable silence blanketed the airwaves for a moment.

"I should get back to work. I'm probably going to stop by Donnie's when I leave the office," said Liam, unable to disguise his aggravation.

"Okay. I'll let you go."

Liam disconnected the call and leaned forward in his chair. He regretted bringing her into his drama. Embarrassed, he placed an elbow on the desk and rested his head in his hand. It would only be a matter of time before Lorraine decided she wanted no part of his crazy, mixed-up family.

Startled by a tap on the door, Liam sat up straight. "Come in."

"I'm headed out." Daisy entered, wearing a smile from ear to ear. Their eyes connected, and a combination of emotions flooded Liam's heart. Guilt was the first to appear. How did he think she was concealing something? Fear followed. What if his mother discovered he questioned her integrity? But those were not the only feelings toying with his mind.

He adored his mother but could not reject the idea that some years ago, she'd have done almost anything for a baby. Did that include manipulating documents to keep a secret? And if she did, what did that mean? She was still his mother, and he still loved her. That would never change. He would do whatever he needed to protect her and her good name.

"Okay. How'd everything go with payroll?" asked Liam.

"Smooth as a baby's bottom." She teased.

"What has you in such a good mood?"

"My son is getting married, so I am gaining a daughter, and a handsome man invited me to dinner."

"Whatever it takes. It's nice to see that smile on your face."

"It would be nice to see one on your face. What's bothering you, son?"

Liam rubbed his temple. Before he replied, Sophia's voice sounded over the intercom. "Mr. Whittington, there is a call on line one for you."

Grateful for the interruption, Liam turned to his mother. "Just last-minute wedding plans. I need to answer this."

"Okay. We'll talk later." Daisy blew an air kiss in his direction and exited without another word.

Liam's heart clogged with guilt. Why did he question his parents? He intended to find out what Curtis was up to. And he hoped it wouldn't cause further damage to the family.

Chapter 20

Later that afternoon, almost everyone had left the Hamilton and Dunn offices. It was almost five o'clock, and most folks had gone for the day or were in the process of leaving. After reviewing the day's notes and highlighting a few follow-up items, Lorraine sat at her desk waiting for Mr. Holloway to come out of a meeting in his office. She wanted to accept the promotion offer before leaving for the day. Her gaze stayed fixed on his closed office door, waiting for the moment it would open. But her mind kept circling back to how unsettled Liam had sounded at the end of their call. A wave of sadness washed over her. The visit to the clerk of courts had uncovered new information. Lorraine couldn't forget what she had discovered. But she couldn't erase the feeling that it made things more complicated for Liam.

Mr. Holloway's door flew open and snapped her back into the present. Kawana Baxter exited and offered Lorraine a polite nod in passing. Returning the gesture, Lorraine pounced out of her chair and trod to the office.

"Mr. Holloway, do you have a minute?"

"Yes."

Lorraine closed the door before sitting in the chair in front of his desk.

"I'd like to accept the senior auditor's position."

"Glad to hear it. I'll start the paperwork first thing in the morning."

"And thanks again for the offer. You won't regret it."

"I'm sure I won't. You're going to make me look like a genius."

"I'll do my best." Lorraine reached across the desk to shake his hand. "I'm done for the day. I'll see you tomorrow, sir."

"All right then. Enjoy your evening."

As soon as she reached her desk, Lorraine logged off the computer and grabbed her things. She shut down the processor, gathered her things, and headed for the door.

Chapter 21

"Can I get a few quarters for laundry?" Curtis tossed a few dollars onto the motel's front office counter. He'd only packed a few clothes, and if he didn't wash them soon, he'd be required to purchase new ones. That wasn't in his budget.

The twenty-something-year-old female flashed a smile, then looked away. "We don't keep cash in here, but you can try the gas station across the street."

Her smile suggested interest, so he turned on the charm.

He offered a playful smirk. "I'm Curtis. What's your name?"

She blushed and giggled. "Oh, I forgot my badge. My name is Maya," she said, rummaging through the desk drawer.

Curtis raised an eyebrow. "You here every evening, Maya?"

"I'm a floater," she said. "I work when they need me."

"Thanks for the heads up about the gas station. Guess I'll head over there later. Meeting a buddy of mine in a few minutes. Mind if I stop by to see you later?"

"I'll be here," she said, pinning the badge on her collar.

Curtis sucked his lips into his mouth, imagining the possibilities. "I'll see you then."

He tossed a wink toward Maya before heading through the door.

Curtis paused in his steps when he noticed a familiar-looking black man walking in his direction. "Boney? Is that you?"

"I told you on the phone that I go by Wayne now."

"Okay, Wayne. It has been a long time."

The two exchanged a one-armed embrace and a tap on the back.

"I see you haven't changed much," said Wayne.

"I don't know what you're talking about, man."

"Yeah, okay. Remember how we used to sneak onto the yard during FAMU homecoming, hoping to hook up with the college girls?"

"That was a while ago."

"Yes, it was," said Wayne, looking off into the distance. "And you always left with some sweet thing on your arm." Wayne shook his shoulders in silent laughter.

"Yeah."

"So glad you called," said Wayne, eyes wide with curiosity.

"Let's talk over there," said Curtis, pointing to just beyond the concrete-covered carport. "I was just about to grab a smoke."

"Great."

Curtis leaned against one of the support poles and lit a cigarette. He held the pack out, offering one to Wayne.

"No, thanks, man. Gave that up a long time ago."

"You still kicking it with Betty Ann?" asked Wayne. "Y'all used to be together all the time."

"No." Curtis rocked his head back and forth. "We eventually got married. But it didn't last. She left me while I was in prison. Took my boys and everything. She got sick and died after that."

"Sorry to hear that, man. We all thought the two of you were a perfect couple?"

"That's why I reached out to you. What have you been up to?" asked Curtis. "Are you still a deejay? I remember you were pretty good at it." He took another drag. The embers flared each time he drew in a breath.

"Yes, I am. Got a good gig coming up. Doing a wedding reception for a young dude. Last name is Whittington."

Curtis' eyelids snapped open in surprise. "Oh, really?" He tilted his head. The corner of his mouth twitched like a man who'd just spotted an opportunity. "Go on. Tell me more."

With intense focus, Curtis hung on to Wayne's every word. He didn't move, didn't interrupt. Just listened to the possibilities. He'd learned to use whatever came his way. But he had received something better than chance. Wayne's unexpected appearance was more than a reunion. It was leverage.

Chapter 22

Day transitioned to evening, spreading warm orange and red hues throughout the sky. Lorraine drove down Apalachee Parkway through the sprinkling of headlights of the busy evening commute. Hands braced against the steering wheel, she rehearsed what she wanted to say to Curtis.

"I'm Lorraine, Liam's fiancée, and I want to know why you're here. What's your agenda? Just leave him alone."

Nothing sounded right, so she made it up as she went along.

She rolled her car into the Motel 6 parking lot. A flash of shame slithered its way through her body. What if someone saw her? Would they assume she was meeting Liam for an early evening rendezvous? She couldn't worry about that now. She needed to uncover Curtis' intentions, or she wouldn't have any kind of rendezvous with Liam.

Lorraine exited the car, pulled her hooded sweater over her head, and sprinted toward the lobby. Maya sat behind the counter, talking on her cell phone.

"Let me call you back. I have a customer," she said before disconnecting the call.

Lorraine pasted on a smile. "Good evening."

"Hi. Can I help you?"

"I hope so. My future father-in-law is staying here. I'd like to surprise him with a visit. Can you tell me which room Curtis Barnes is in?"

"They don't allow us to give out room numbers."

Tilting her head, Lorraine gave a curt giggle. "I suppose people come and go so fast around here, right? I'd never keep track."

"Yeah. But I can tell you there is no smoking in the building. If he were a smoker, he'd probably be hanging around outside somewhere." She stared straight ahead, chewing slowly.

"Okay …," It took a few seconds for Lorraine to catch on, but she realized the receptionist had dropped a hint. "Oh … okay. Thank you."

Lorraine exited the lobby.

So, what am I supposed to do with that information? Walk around the building looking for smokers? And then what? I have no idea what Curtis looks like. But I know he's an angry man with little to no boundaries. If I confronted him, how would he react? No one knows I'm here. He could beat me up, throw me in one of those dumpsters, or something like that. This was a bad idea. Besides, it's chilly and dark, I'm not getting snatched up. Not tonight.

Warding off the nip, Lorraine drew her sweater tighter and slipped her head into the hoodie. She looked around and noticed two men standing near the corner beneath the overhead lights. One man stood with his back to her; the other faced her with a lit cigarette dangling from his mouth. The cancer stick shook as he spoke. They appeared to be arguing. It was difficult to tell, but one of them looked familiar, though she couldn't place him.

What if he's someone from church or a former client? What if he recognizes me? Maybe I should go the other way? If I do that, I'll have to walk all the way around the building to get to my car. Who knows what's lurking on the other side?

She adjusted the hoodie's drawstring tighter around her face and trudged. The quiet hum of streetlights softened her measured steps. The men's angry voices sliced through the silence. She tried to seem relaxed, pretending to check her phone. Her heart beat louder with each of their exchanged words.

"Look, Curtis, I'm gonna do it, but I'm not responsible for the outcome."

Lorraine took a sharp breath when she heard the name Curtis. Could this be Liam's biological father? She caught her breath as the pieces came together. The arguing continued.

"I'll pay you to do it."

"I'm going to need more than you're offering. Folks 'round here love Daisy Whittington. Besides, those boys will believe nothing negative about their mother."

"She's not their mother. And I don't care if they believe it or not. I just want them to doubt her."

Lorraine quickened her steps. Fixing her eyes ahead, she straightened her posture. Not enough to draw attention. Just enough to escape.

Safe beyond their periphery, she sprinted to the car. She fumbled for the key fob, hands trembling not just from the cold, but from distress.

***

Lorraine drove out of the parking lot, leaving the vicious, plot-scheming men behind. She found a well-lit area at a nearby Walgreens and parked her car. With trembling hands, she retrieved her phone and tapped on Liam's name from her favorites. He didn't answer, so she hung up and sent a text: WE NEED TO TALK.

This man is not only planning to disrupt our wedding, but to put Liam's mother on front street. What kind of man does this to his son? This can't be happening. It sounds like a soap opera episode.

She tossed the phone onto the passenger seat and rubbed her shaky hands together.

What if they had recognized me? Neither of them seemed to have scruples. There's no telling what they would have done to me to keep their dirty little secret. Thank God for that hoodie.

After a few moments of self-reflection, Lorraine tried to reach Liam again. No answer.

I know he was upset when we spoke earlier, but it's not like him to ignore my calls. If he's worked up now, he's really going to be worked up when I tell him about this escapade. I don't have a choice. I have to tell him. He needs to know what Curtis is planning.

Chapter 23

With everyone gone for the day, Liam took advantage of the quiet time to read the daily log submitted by foreman, Alan Davis. Once they secured final approval for the tree trimming, the E & G project could begin work. He uploaded photos and made notes for site preparation and tree removal.

Liam logged out of his computer and started shutting down the office. That's when Curtis' words blasted in his mind.

"You're no better than me. Watch and see. In a few years, you'll be just like me. No kids, no wife, and no family."

What if everything he said is true?

Lorraine deserves better.

There was only one other person who would understand his concern. He needed to talk to Donnie. But first, he needed to apologize for the abrupt way he had left things earlier that day.

"Hello," Donnie answered with an even tone.

"Hey, bro. I owe you an apology for this afternoon. My bad. I'm having a tough time figuring things out right now."

"The wheel has come full circle," said Donnie, quoting King Lear.

"I do not talk like Shakespeare."

"In other words, we're back to square one."

"I guess so. I understand it's Friday night and that you likely have plans; however, do you have time for a fast visit?"

"No problem. I'm on my way home now."

"I'll pick up a couple of burgers and meet you there."

Less than thirty minutes later, the two sat at Donnie's kitchen table, scoffing down Whataburger meals.

"Two visits in one day. What makes me so special? Shouldn't you and Lorraine be somewhere going over wedding plans?" asked Donnie, chomping on an onion ring.

"We probably should. She called me on my way over here, but I didn't pick up."

"Trouble in paradise?"

Liam rubbed the back of his neck. "Actually, Curtis is the one causing all the trouble. And somehow, Lorraine got caught in the middle of it."

"That's because Curtis placed her there. She's probably upset because he threatened to disrupt the wedding." Donnie took a huge bite of his burger.

Liam stared at Donnie. "I still haven't shared that part with her."

"Man …"

"I don't want to drag her into my drama," he said dryly. "But she keeps inserting herself."

"That's because she loves you, bro."

"I know that, but she deserves better." Liam paused before continuing. "Lorraine went to the clerk of the courts' office today."

"And?"

Liam relayed Lorraine's visit with the clerk and everything that transpired.

"We got him!" Donnie released a wide grin before taking another chunk of his burger.

"Not necessarily," said Liam. "We don't know that for certain. Anyone could have accessed the file."

"Who else could it be?" Donnie shook his head as if to erase what he heard. He sank back into his chair, nostrils flaring. "Please tell me you don't think it was Mom?"

Liam shrugged. "What if she thought it would protect us from something? Don't you think she would do it?"

Donnie pushed away from the table and walked across the room. "Look, I will not sit here and argue with you about whether our mother would manipulate government records. I'm just not going to do it!"

Silence.

Not a sound.

Just the echo of Donnie's words.

Suddenly, the doorbell rang, breaking the quiet.

"Answer the door. We're done here," said Liam, waving a hand in the air.

"No, we're not. We need to decide what to do about Curtis. I say we call his bluff."

Liam took a minute to gather himself. He wasn't sure he could control his temper if he were ever in the same room with Curtis again. "I don't know if that is a good idea."

The doorbell rang once more.

"You may as well answer it. Whoever it is, they're not going away," barked Liam, annoyed by the interruption.

Donnie made his way to the front door and pulled it open.

Lorraine stood on the other side.

Chapter 24

"Lorraine, it's nice to see you. Come on in," said Donnie.

Stepping over the threshold, she offered a hug and an apology. "Forgive me for dropping by without warning. I've been trying to reach Liam, but he won't answer his phone. I thought he might be here. His car is in the driveway, so I was right."

Donnie closed the door behind Lorraine. "He's here feeding his face."

Lorraine smiled and followed him to the kitchen.

Liam glanced up from the table, lifting a brow. "What are you doing here?"

For an anxious moment, they locked eyes. The air between them swelled with a suppressed tension that neither wanted to address. "I called your cell, but it forwarded to voicemail."

"Lorraine, can I get you something to eat or drink?" asked Donnie.

"No. Thank you."

"I'll get out of the way so you two can talk." Donnie eyed Liam for confirmation.

Lorraine tilted her head toward Donnie. "You don't have to leave. You're both going to want to hear what I have to say. Then I'll be on my way."

"What is it?" asked Liam, pushing away from the table. He stood and pulled out the chair next to where he had been sitting. After placing a gentle kiss on her cheek, he gestured for her to sit.

"Stay as long as you like." Donnie sat on the other side of Lorraine.

"What's up?" asked Liam.

Lorraine regrouped. "I have something to say, and neither of you will like it. But I was just trying to help."

"What did you do?" Liam pinched the bridge of his nose. He looked worried and determined.

"I went to Motel 6 to speak with Curtis," she said, scarcely looking at either of them.

Liam snapped. "You did what?"

Donnie shook his head. "Lorraine?"

"Listen to me." "I arrived at the motel, but they wouldn't share his room number with me."

Liam rose and walked to the other side of the kitchen before stopping to lean against the counter. "So, you didn't see him?"

"I saw him, but I didn't speak with him." Her voice trembled as she described what she'd witnessed in the parking lot.

Liam punched a fist in the air, his rising frustration palpable.

"It sounds like his beef is with Mom, and he's using you to do it," Donnie said to him.

"You're right," barked Liam.

"And that's why he wants an invitation to the wedding." The words slipped from Donnie's lips before he could stop them.

"He wants an invitation to the wedding?" Lorraine snapped her head in Liam's direction, her anger simmering just below the surface. "Why didn't you tell me?"

An awkward pause ensued.

"I just remembered something I need to take care of," said Donnie, pushing away from the table before forcing a hasty retreat.

Liam took a deep breath. "You had enough on your mind. I didn't want to add to it."

Lorraine stood, eyes narrowed in confusion. "But you promised … We promised. No secrets. You should have said something."

Liam folded his arms across his chest. His eyes landed on hers. "I guess we both broke promises to each other."

She would never admit it to him. But he had a point. Instead, she grabbed her purse and pivoted toward the door.

"We should delay the wedding," Liam said, his voice low but underlain with tension.

Pressing a hand to her chest, Lorraine turned. She took a small step forward. Her voice softened. "You're scaring me, Liam. Just tell me what's really going on."

Liam stood completely still. His shoulders squared, hands at his side like a soldier delivering unwanted orders.

Lorraine's shoulders sank as the weight of the last few months settled in. She didn't want to agree with him.

Postpone the wedding? Maybe we should. The past four months have taken a toll. Every slight disagreement has grown into something bigger. We've been drifting even when standing side-by-side. Were we too eager to marry?

Her eyes, damp with unshed tears, finally meet his. She offered a reluctant surrender. "You're right. Perhaps we should delay the wedding."

Liam reached for her hand. She pulled away, resisting the urge to fall into his arms.

Lorraine stomped out of the door and headed to her car. Once inside, the tears came cascading down like a rapid waterfall. Squinting through the tears, she started the engine, placed the car in gear, and raced down the street.

Chapter 25

Bam!

The door slammed shut, and Donnie came hurrying from the back of the townhouse. His eyes wide, bewilderment unfolded across his face. "What happened?"

Liam stood in the kitchen, his thoughts revolving around Lorraine and the hurt in her eyes. "She's gone."

Donnie looked stunned. When he finally replied, he said. "You just gonna let her leave like that?"

Liam took one step back, his voice low and firm. "The wedding is off, for now."

"You just gonna give up?" asked Donnie, flailing his hands in concern.

Liam took a deep breath, steadying himself. "I don't have a choice. I said some things I shouldn't have said."

"Then apologize!" Donnie's eyes flashed with annoyance.

Curtis's words resonated in Liam's head like a warning he couldn't unhear. *"You're no better than I am. Watch and see. In a few years, you'll be just like me. No kids, no wife, and no family."*

"I don't know if I'm ready?"

"What do you mean?"

"I don't know if I can be the husband Lorraine's deserves."

Donnie placed a calming hand on his shoulder. "Where's all this coming from?"

"They taught us we find our identity in Christ."

"Yeah."

Liam's stomach knotted as he stared into space. "But with all the lies about our adoption, I don't know who I am. If the foundation of my adoption … our adoption is shaky, what do we really know about ourselves?"

Donnie leaned into his brother, radiating compassion. "Nothing changes who we are in Christ. That's solid. I'm not sure of the exact verse, but the Scripture says, 'we are His workmanship, created in Christ Jesus unto good works, which God hath before ordained that we should walk in them.'"

Liam stood, looking back at Donnie. "I know the Scriptures, bro! But I'm also the son of a man who threatened to sabotage his own son's wedding. He's been in and out of jail. He's a lifetime criminal. What if I turn out to be like him?"

"Who are you to disagree with what God says about you?" asked Donnie with conviction. "You're falling for a lie. Now ask yourself where the lie is coming from? Remember, we wrestle not against flesh and blood. So, who is lying to you, bro?"

Liam felt a glimmer of hope as the weight on his shoulders eased. He appreciated Donnie's compassion.

"Satan."

Donnie grabbed Liam's shoulder with a firm hand. "We already know that his job is to steal, kill, and destroy. Maybe he knows what the two of you could accomplish for the Kingdom of God. What better way to destroy your purpose than to use Curtis to do the dirty work?"

Chapter 26

Standing at her front door, the sting of tears blurred the keypad, but Lorraine persisted. She stabbed at the watery haze, missing numbers she'd punched a hundred times before.

Suddenly, the door flew open, and Dee appeared. One look at Lorraine and she asked, "Why are you crying? What happened to you?"

"Why are you meeting me at the front door? Were you waiting for me or something?" Lorraine rushed in, threw her purse on the coffee table, and slumped on the couch.

Dee followed, hands flailing. "No, I heard you struggling with the keypad, so I came to let you in. What happened?"

"Sorry for barking at you," said Lorraine, gaining her composure.

"No problem." Dee sat next to Lorraine, wrapping a sympathetic arm around her shoulders. "What has you so upset?"

Tears gathered in Lorraine's eyes like rain caught in a windowpane. She blinked hard, trying to restrain the impending overflow.

"Liam and I had a huge argument … and … we postponed the wedding." Her voice broke with every word. And so did the dam that held back the tears. They came in erratic waves, each faster than the last. She tried to stop crying, but the momentum of it all dragged her under.

Dee drew her near and held Lorraine through every heartbreaking moment. And when Lorraine felt like coming up for air, she was there to let her breathe. No questions. No words. Just there to comfort her friend. When Lorraine finally spoke, her voice trembled.

Dee listened to every word.

"I'm so sorry, honey. Do you suppose its pre-wedding jitters? It's common, you know."

Lorraine sat up straight and turned toward Dee.

"Could be," she said, between sniffles. "But you'd think we'd be able to handle it considering all the things we learned in counseling."

Lorraine dabbed a tear from her cheek. She assumed Dee would offer to pray about the situation because when trouble stirred, she fell on her knees. When that didn't happen, she continued, "I wanted to help so I did something."

"Like what?" Dee's eyes widened.

"I went to see Curtis at Motel 6."

"Lorraine, if Curtis is causing trouble for his sons, what makes you think he wouldn't cause trouble for you? Or possibly even hurt you physically. He didn't, did he?"

"No. I'm fine. But evidently, Liam didn't appreciate my help."

"Did he ask for your help?"

Lorraine tossed her hands up in frustration. "Are you seriously taking Liam's side?"

"I'm not taking anyone's side. But I can see why Liam wouldn't want your help. He's probably embarrassed."

Tears welled up in Lorraine's eyes as the thought besieged her.

Dee extended a tender smile. "You guys should talk to each other, maybe after you've both cooled off."

"I don't know if he'll ever talk to me again." She looked off into the distance.

"Have you seen the way he looks at you? That man loves you. Love like that doesn't just fade away when there's an argument. Let me pray with you," said Dee.

Despite her earlier frustration, Lorraine welcomed the offer. "I'd like that."

With hands joined and heads bowed, Dee offered a prayer.

Lorraine's heart swelled with gratitude. She hoped things would work out for Liam and her. But if they didn't, she knew she would be all right in her Heavenly Father's arms.

Chapter 27

Lorraine looked in her bathroom mirror the following morning and grimaced. Sleeplessness was clear in the red-rimmed, heavy, puffy eyes. Her hair was messy, and her cracked lips trembled as if she were deciding whether to cry or smile. She could hardly recognize herself; she appeared both weak and resilient, as though pain had weakened her but hadn't fully broken her.

Is this what love leaves behind? Her fingertips gently touched the bags under her eyes. *A woman who barely recognizes herself?*

Her chest ached, and she feared she would cry again. But then the thought stilled. *You've survived heartbreak before. Even though you feel shaky, you're still standing.*

Her chest rose with a shaky breath, not strong enough to steady her, but not weak enough to undo her. Liam might have been right. Maybe pressing pause isn't failure—it's mercy. Maybe God's timing asks for patience, even when my heart wants to rush ahead.

Lorraine pressed her palm to the mirror, anchoring herself. The woman staring back at her wasn't who she wanted to see, but she was still here. Weary, yes. Frayed at the edges. But not undone. *This isn't the end of you,* she reminded herself, though her voice inside trembled. God's not finished even if you don't see the way forward yet.

Her reflection blinked back at her, a mixture of defeat and the faintest flicker of resolve. Not despair. Not peace. Just somewhere in between—waiting, breathing, holding on.

After taking a shower and dressing, she headed for her parents'
home. It would be a tough conversation, but she needed to deal with
it so they could take the next steps. She gave herself a pep-talk as she
drove down Thomasville Road.

*You can do this, Lorraine. Dad and Mom have spent a lot of money on
this wedding. I know Dad will be upset about that. Hopefully, we'll be able to
mitigate the damage before it's too late. Maybe I'll talk to Mom alone first. She'll
understand and relay everything to Dad later. She'll have questions, of course. I'll
answer what I can. But Mom will know what I should do and how I should do it.
I'll offer to help with the cost, of course. Which she will refuse, but I'll offer. But
most importantly, I can't cry—no more tears.*

"Dad's here," she said, noticing his vehicle parked in the
driveway. "I'll have to steal a few moments alone with Mom."

She heard her mother's voice as soon as she walked through
the front door. "You look beautiful in your dress. Aunt Lorraine is
going to love it."

*She must be chatting with Clarrissa on the phone. They're probably
referring to Clarrissa's flower girl dresses. It must have arrived. She will be
disappointed when she finds out the wedding is delayed.*

Lorraine paused in the entryway as tears threatened to fall.

"Baby girl! Come on in. I thought I heard someone entering."
Her father appeared from around the corner, wearing a smile that
stretched from ear to ear.

Lorraine stepped into his welcoming arms, feeling his quiet
strength, and the weight of her grief.

"Hi, Daddy," she said, burying her pain. "How are you?"

"Doing pretty good for an old man. Your mother's in the kitchen, on the phone. Have you had breakfast?"

"No. But I'm not hungry."

"Well, you know your mother will not let you get away without feeding you. She made grits and eggs. Go on in there and get some."

"Thanks, Dad."

"I've got an appointment to get some new tires for my truck. Shouldn't take more than an hour. Will you be here when I get back?"

"Maybe."

"You and Liam have plans for the day?"

"No, sir. I have some other things I need to take care of."

"Okay. Then go get you some breakfast out the kitchen. I'm gonna change my shoes," said Dr. Davis, heading to the back of the house.

Sunlight edged through the kitchen blinds, painting warm stripes across the floor. The smell of brewing coffee mingled with the faint aroma of bacon. Lorraine stepped inside and eased herself into the chair at the table.

"Okay, uh-huh. That's great." Her mother's voice floated through the room, bright, and cheerful as she waved frantically to say hello.

Lorraine smiled and made herself a cup of coffee. Fixing her gaze on the steam rising from her coffee mug, she willed herself not to cry. The heat curled upward, unfocused like her thoughts.

Maybe I should call him. The thought struck, sudden and uninvited. *All I want is to hear his voice. Just to say I didn't mean it like that.*

Just to ask if he's hurting too. Or maybe I should let it be. Enjoy spending time with my parents. Anything but let him hear me like this.

Helen disconnected the call, then turned her attention to her daughter with a bright, expectant smile. "Hey, Lorraine. You don't look happy this morning. Is everything okay?"

Lorraine forced a small smile. For a few minutes, she just sat there, breathing, holding herself together, counting each heartbeat, and each small comfort—the sunlight, the smell of breakfast, her mother's laughter lingering in the air. She didn't cry, not yet. She just let herself exist in that fragile balance between sorrow and the gentle pull of everyday life, hoping that eventually, the ache would soften, even if only slightly.

Lorraine fixed her eyes on the pot of grits warming on the stove, blinking hard to clear the blur that threatened. Her throat burned, an ache that came just before tears spilled. She pressed her lips together, but the tremor in her chin gave her away. When her mother glanced over, still smiling from the phone call, Lorraine lowered her eyes, whispering inside, *Lord, help me keep it together.*

"What brings you by early this morning?" Her father's cheerful baritone voice snapped her out of her misery.

She sniffled, gathered her thoughts, and said, "Thought I'd drop by before starting my errands."

More like I needed to talk to you guys before I started making phone calls to postpone the wedding.

Helen glanced from Lorraine to her husband before landing a side-eye on Lorraine. They narrowed with concern.

She knows something's wrong. Lorraine lowered her gaze.

"James, you'd better hurry, or you'll be late," said Helen.

"You're right," he said, walking over to Helen, kissing her on the cheek. "I'll be back in a little bit."

"See you later, Dad. Love you."

"Love you, too," said James and walked out the door.

Helen stepped toward Lorraine. "What's wrong, Lorraine?"

"Liam and I postponed the wedding."

Her knees almost buckled. The second her mother's arms enclosed around her, Lorraine sank. Holding tight, with her face buried in the familiar curve of her mother's shoulder: Vanilla, Dove's beauty bar, home. The scents wrapped around her as certainly as the embrace.

Sobs pelted, one after another, until her body shuddered with the force of them. She felt her mother's palm edge over her back, a steady rhythm quieting the panic beating in her ribs.

Her thoughts muddled with the sound of her own crying and the hushed pound of her mother's heart under her ear. She held on, breathing in shattered gasps. Slowly, the sobs allayed, retreating into minor tremors, then into silence.

Rushing to the living room, Helen grabbed a box of tissues from the side table and handed a few to Lorraine.

"Mom, I am so sorry. I know you and Dad have spent a lot of money on the wedding. I promise I will …"

"Don't even go there. The important thing is for you to be sure. Why do you want to postpone the wedding?"

"I think we may have rushed things."

"I don't want you to confuse cold feet with a divine warning. Take the time to know which it is, and He'll give you peace about it."

I want peace. I need peace. But everything seems jumbled and loud. Do I really know Liam? Do I even know myself?

"A wedding is just a day, but a marriage is a lifetime. Don't step into forever unless you can say yes with your whole heart," said Helen, reaching for Lorraine's hand. "You don't have to prove anything to anyone. Not me. Not your father, not the guests, not the world. The only approval you need is God's."

The words sank in, wrapping around the panic coiled in her chest. *Am I running or am I meant to step back?*

"Are you afraid of the man, or are you afraid of the promise? The difference matters. Ask God about it."

Lorraine closed her eyes, letting herself hear the ticking clock, feel the warmth of her mother's touch, smell the faint trace of coffee. The memories, the doubts, the fears were all still there, but something deeper stirred beneath them. *God is bigger than all of this.*

Her shoulders loosened. Breath came easier. For the first time, she leaned into waiting.

Chapter 28

Sunday night, Liam lay in the calm of his bedroom with the Bible in his hand. The week had been a series of contentious encounters. Not only had he met and fought his biological father, but he'd also estranged his brother and probably lost his fiancée. Now alone in his room, he searched the Scriptures for answers.

After reflecting on Ephesians chapter two verse ten, Liam dozed off with the Bible next to him in bed. Images from the tumultuous week flashed through his mind. He saw visions of the hateful look in Curtis's eyes as he prophesied failure over his life, marriage, and posterity.

"You're no better than I am. Watch and see. In a few years, you'll be just like me. No kids, no wife, and no family."

He could not relax, kicking the covers, only to draw them back. He tossed and turned, unable to rest. One minute, Curtis's words echoed; the next minute, God's words resonated: "we are his workmanship, created in Christ Jesus unto good works, which God hath before ordained that we should walk in them."

He struggled to decide which report to trust.

Liam woke the next morning with twisted sheets and a sweaty pillowcase. His mouth ached from clenching his jaw during the night. Then suddenly, a familiar verse pierced his thoughts like a bloom that opened overnight.

"We wrestle not against flesh and blood, but against principalities, against powers, against the rulers of darkness of this world, against spiritual wickedness in high places."

Reaching for his Bible, Liam flipped through the book of Ephesians until he found chapter 6:12. He read it out loud, then talked himself through it.

"We, the believers, that's me. I'm not wrestling against Lorraine or Curtis. It's the rulers of darkness. Why would the rulers of darkness want to cause trouble for me and Lorraine? Why would they want to bring Curtis into my life with all his lies? And why now?"

He couldn't sit still for another second. He hurled the covers from his body and dropped to the floor. Push-ups first, hard, and fast. Then sit-ups, one after the other.

Push through!

Dig deep!

One more rep!

Liam pushed himself until his muscles burned. At least he could understand the pain. He pulled his sweat-drenched body into the shower. Leaning against the tile, he bowed his head.

"Lord, I understand I'm not fighting flesh and blood. I get that. But what am I supposed to do? I postponed my wedding because I didn't want Curtis there. Now I may have lost the love of my life. Please tell me what to do, and I promise I'll do it."

In that moment, under the pounding of hot, dripping water, Liam realized he desperately needed the Lord. He'd promised to obey

God. Did he fulfill that vow, or had he merely prayed himself into difficulty?

***

Later that morning, Liam followed the aroma of coffee into the kitchen. Lingering near the entrance, he watched his mother break a few eggs and drop them into a bowl. Maybe he could stall for a few minutes before telling her about postponing the wedding. But knowing his mother, she'd be able to see through his smiling face and detect his anxiety.

He placed a hand on her shoulder. "Good morning."

"Good morning," she said, scrambling the eggs. "Thought I'd make breakfast for us before I left for church."

I should tell her now.

Liam leaned against the counter. "About that …."

"Sorry for interrupting," she said, waving a finger in the air. "But I need to tell you before I forget. Cousin Bonita called yesterday. Uncle Lemuel is in the hospital. He will stay there briefly before entering rehab. They can't make it to the wedding. She apologized for the late notice."

Daisy took a sip of coffee from the cup next to the stove.

"I'm sorry to hear that he's sick, but there's something I need to tell you."

Daisy poured the eggs into the pan and watched them cook for a few seconds.

Liam pulled a stool from the bar and sat down.

Their eyes met, and Daisy's expression changed. A trace of worry crossed her features. "What is it?"

After contemplating for a moment, he said, "Lorraine and I are postponing the wedding."

"Why? What happened?"

Liam shook his head. "I prefer not to discuss it."

Daisy examined him for a long moment; her look was pointed and assessing.

He was aware of her ability to see through him.

"Whose idea was it to postpone the wedding?"

With irritation festering, Liam wiped his hands over his face. "Mine."

"Are you having cold feet, or did something happen?" She pressed.

He wanted to pour out his heart to his mother while holding parts back for himself. After struggling all night with his feelings about Lorraine and Curtis, he'd asked God for direction. The problem was that he knew his mother's advice would likely align with what God said. And he wasn't ready to receive verbal confirmation.

"Mom," he muttered, clenched his fist, and crushed his lips shut.

"You realize that if you delay the wedding, there's a chance you could lose Lorraine. You said you believed she was the woman God set apart for you."

Dropping his head, Liam closed his eyes. "I still believe that."

Daisy removed the pan from the heat, then placed the eggs on a platter. After washing and drying her hands, she stood across from him at the kitchen counter.

"Talk to me." Her voice softened. "Tell me what you're feeling. Of course, I don't want you to get married if you're not ready. And I will support you in that. But postponing the wedding is a big step. Both emotionally and financially. Have you thought about that?"

"Yes, I have. But I don't have a choice. There's no way around it."

Twisting her mouth, Daisy seemed pensive. "Is there a third party involved?"

"What?"

"Does this involve another man or woman?"

Liam couldn't lie to his mother. "There is another man involved."

"I'm surprised. Are you sure?"

He inhaled, and a knot rose in his chest.

She thinks Lorraine cheated. She's way off base. I can't let her think that. Things are already out of control.

"Lorraine's not cheating on me," explained Liam.

"I don't understand. Just spit it out," she said, tapping her foot with impatience.

"I need to tell you something, and you will not like it."

"What is it, Liam? You're making me nervous," she said, eyes wide open.

"It's Curtis Barnes." Liam waited for his mother's reaction before continuing. She looked at him with a combination of concern and helplessness. He knew his words affected her.

Daisy didn't respond immediately; instead, she stared into the distance. "How does Curtis factor in this?"

Then, with a loud groan, Liam told her every ugly little detail.

An unnerving quiet filled the room.

"I hope you don't put faith in him," she said, squeezing her lips in frustration. "I despise his behavior, and I am sorry that you couldn't seek help from me. I'm happy to answer questions you and your brother have about the adoption. The records are in your father's office. You are welcome to read them whenever."

"I'm sorry, Mom. I should never have doubted you."

Daisy shifted her body forward. "How does this tie into wedding postponement?"

"At first, it was because I didn't want Curtis to disrupt the ceremony. I didn't want to give him the opportunity to broadcast his lies."

"We can handle that." She gave him an encouraging smile. "We'll have someone posted at every entrance. I'm sure Lorraine's friend, Brandon, will be happy to help with that. Curtis won't get in. Anyway, people are going to believe what they want to believe anyway."

Liam rolled his shoulders backward. "How do you do that? How do you just move on? I can't. I want to hurt Curtis for everything he's done to and said about you. How do I move past that?"

"Forgive him," said Daisy with calm assurance.

"You're asking a lot, Mom."

"I'm not asking you to do anything." Daisy rose from her seat, reached for her cup, and started the Keurig. "I'm telling you what God requires. You can do it or not. But there are consequences either way. It's up to you."

"I know. Donnie basically said the same thing."

"And he was right."

"Every time I feel like I can forgive the man, he says or does something else, and I'm angry all over again."

"How do your feelings relate to God's directives?" Daisy spoke with clear conviction, lacking any doubt.

"Nothing." He shrugged his shoulders.

Liam contemplated his mother's words. Unfortunately, she was telling the truth. Liam understood that forgiveness wouldn't come easily, yet he desired to forgive Curtis.

"With that cleared up, why is the wedding postponed?"

Liam's chest tightened. The words came out before he could reel them in.

"I have a memory of riding in Dad's truck after a late game. The streetlights flickering across the windshield are something I remember. I was about sixteen years old. Anyway, I didn't play very well that night, and I sat sulking in after a tough basketball loss, still sweaty and sore. Dad tossed me a towel." He asked me whether I thought he cared about the score. Of course, I said yes.

"What matters to me is you got back up every time you fell," he said. "A father's job is the same. Keep getting back up for your kids, no matter what."

Liam looked into his mother's eyes. "I'm scared, Mom." His voice cracked, low. "What if I turn out to be like Curtis?"

The confession hung heavy between them. Liam dropped his head into his hands.

Daisy's eyebrows soared to her hairline. "What makes you think you'll be like Curtis?"

"I guess it goes back to the nurture versus nature argument. Father embodied a fine example of fatherhood. I want to be like him," said Liam.

"Harold, though wonderful, possessed flaws. He would have been the first to admit he had made mistakes. Instead, he tried to emulate the Heavenly Father, for He is perfect."

Liam stared straight ahead. "This morning, I sought God's guidance. I think I have my answer."

Daisy smirked, pointing a finger at her chest. "I think there's something else you need to do."

"Apologize to Lorraine."

"Yes, sir. And do it quickly before she makes phone calls to postpone the wedding."

Chapter 29

Liam slammed his hand against the steering wheel and shouted, "Pick up the phone. Come on, baby. Pick up the phone."

He disconnected the call and continued down Thomasville Road to Lorraine's condominium. It was still early morning. She had to be home. If not, he would track her down. He had to.

Turning into the complex, he breathed a sigh of relief when he spotted her car. He swerved into an empty spot and jumped out. Taking two steps at a time, he scaled the stairs like an Olympic sports climber. Mounting the platform and sprinting to the door.

"Lorraine, please. I need to talk to you!" he panted, poking the doorbell like it owed him something.

No answer.

He pounded his fist on the door. "Please, Lorraine. We need to talk. I'm sorry."

It screeched open as if it were trying to decide whether it even wanted to deal with him. And then she appeared.

Lorraine stood in the doorway, gawking at him beneath a monstrous, shiny pink bonnet that sat on her head like a crown made of cotton candy. A layer of silky white cream covered her face. A fuzzy yellow robe nearly swallowed her whole, cinched tight at the waist like it was hanging on for dear life.

Liam's mouth flew open, then closed again.

"I'm so sorry," he said, just above a whisper.

She raised an eyebrow but said nothing. Then she moved aside. "Come in before you wake the neighbors."

He nodded, walking inside. The door clicked shut behind them.

They stood in the entrance, just inches apart, arms firm at their sides. Neither said a word. The silence shouted with everything they hadn't said and the utter ridiculousness of the moment.

Liam eyeballed her bonnet. Lorraine's eyes dropped to her fuzzy slippers.

And then, suddenly, she snorted—a tiny, unexpected sound.

He chuckled.

She tried to hold hers back. Too late.

The laughter hit them both like an uncontrollable ripple. They gave in to it, shoulders shaking, breath catching, laughing not just at how outrageous she looked, but at how much they needed this break in the storm.

Liam turned to see a Dee lumbering in, prepared to attack. With rollers stacked high, and a paisley robe fastened over plaid pajamas, she held a slipper in one hand like a weapon.

"What in the world is going on out here?" her voice sharp and full of angst.

She noticed Lorraine's cream-covered face and Liam's nervous grin. Both doubled over in laughter.

Dee paused with both hands on her hips.

Then she released a loud sigh. "I thought somebody was breaking in. Y'all in here cackling like hyenas."

Dee gave them the once-over, then cracked a smile.

And with a deep, contagious laugh, she joined in.

After gaining their composure, Dee backed away. "I don't know what you two are going through. But I'm going to my room. Good morning to both of you. Lorraine, call me if you need me."

"Thanks, Dee," said Lorraine.

"Good morning to you," said Liam, following Lorraine into the living room.

"Have a seat. I'll be right back," she said before walking to her bedroom.

With mixed emotions, he collapsed onto the sofa. He was grateful for the impromptu laugh fest, but anxious about what he needed to say to Lorraine.

She returned a few minutes later wearing a clean face, combed hair, sweatpants, and a t-shirt. She stood in front of him and handed him a piece of paper with a list of names and numbers. "I've written every vendor we need to contact. I'll take the first half, and you can take the second half. There'll be cancellation fees. I think we should split them. You should have the names of the people on your guest list. If you contact yours, I'll contact mine."

Liam flailed a hand in the air. "No. Wait one second."

"Why? This is a fair way to get it done. What don't you agree with?"

"Please. Let's talk."

She dropped her shoulders. "What's left to talk about?"

"I know I have no right to ask, but please sit down and listen?" He added and pressed his palms to his chest. "Hear me out. Then I promise to leave if you want me to."

With guarded steps, she walked to the other end of the sofa. She sat with her arms folded across her chest and legs crossed at the ankles.

"Lorraine, have you …" he looked into her eyes and knew he would do anything to spend the rest of his life with her. He couldn't understand why he'd pushed her away. He just prayed she would give him another chance. "Have you started making any of these calls yet?"

"You came here at this time of the morning to ask me that?" Lorraine's eyebrows arched so high they almost reached her hairline. "No, I haven't. I planned to start on Monday. If I'm moving too slow for you, why don't you start? You have the names of all the points of contact."

Liam shook his head in disbelief. "No, I don't want to."

"Neither do I." Her hands flew to her chest. "But someone has to do it."

"Wait." He leaned closer toward her with hands open and palms up. "That's not what I meant. I was trying to say I don't want to postpone the wedding. I want to get married as planned."

Lorraine leaned back and rested her hands calmly in her lap. "That's great, but I haven't changed my mind. Marriage isn't just about vows. It's about walking through life together. But I can't walk with you if you keep shutting me out."

Liam opened his mouth to argue, then quickly smacked it closed. She spoke the truth, and he knew it.

He turned to face her. "You're right. I was confused. I didn't want to be like Curtis. He's not my idea of a good man, and I have his genetics. I didn't want to bring you into all of that. You and our future children deserve better."

Lorraine raised her hand, stopping him. "Don't you see, you could never be like him. You're the kindest, sweetest, most thoughtful man I know." Tears fell from her eyes.

They studied each other for an intense moment. Liam didn't breathe, and he was confident Lorraine didn't either. The sensation between them overflowed with love and understanding.

"Thank you, babe. I know now that my identity is not in my biological dad. It's not even in my adopted father. My identity is in my Heavenly Father. I am who He says I am. And He says I am His heir and joint heir with Christ."

"True," said Lorraine, restraining a smile. "You are a good man."

"I'm sorry I didn't open up to you. Sharing my feelings isn't something that comes naturally for me. But I know it's important, so I will try to do better. Will you forgive me?"

"Yes, of course."

"Can we please not postpone the wedding?"

"What about Curtis and your mother?"

"I prayed long and hard last night and this morning. I prayed about Mom, Curtis, you, and me. Now I have clarity. I talked to Mom.

You and Donnie were right. Curtis was lying about everything. I asked Mom to forgive me for doubting her, and she did. I asked you to forgive me, and you did. And Curtis? I asked God to help me forgive him. And He's working with me on that."

They laughed together, low and easy, like a secret only their hearts understood.

Liam pulled her closer. He held on as if it could be their last time together. Using both thumbs, he gently wiped away her tears.

"Liam," she whispered.

The way she breathed his name sent his heart racing. Unable to resist, Liam lowered his mouth to hers. He kissed her with a penetrating thirst and desire for more.

He heard Dee's footsteps thundering down the hall and immediately remembered they weren't alone … or married. Liam pulled his arms away from Lorraine as if he had been caught eating a cookie before dinner.

Dee entered the living room, still draped in pajamas and a robe, minus the rollers.

"What brings you back in here?" asked Liam. His tone was flustered and guilty.

Dee tilted her head and smirked. "Oh, I'm sorry. Did I interrupt your lustful temptation?"

Giggling, Lorraine grabbed Liam's hand. "No worries. He was about to leave."

"Just doing my part to protect the wedding night storyline," said Dee. Smiling, she walked toward the kitchen.

Liam turned to Lorraine. "So, we're good?"

"We're good."

He retrieved the list from the sofa and ripped it into pieces. "Would you mind putting this where it belongs?"

"I'd be happy to." Lorraine removed the pieces from his palm and wadded them with her fist. Together they strolled to the front door.

"Thanks for the interruption, Dee!" he yelled into the kitchen. "As always, your timing is impeccable."

Dee shouted back, "Not my timing. You know what they say, He may not come when you want Him …"

"But He's always on time." The trio recited in unison.

After a soft kiss to Lorraine's lips, Liam stepped out the door and headed to his vehicle.

Chapter 30

Despite his feelings, Liam drove down Thomasville Road toward Apalachee Parkway. A man who threatened to ruin the wedding and defame his mother had no place in his life. Not now and not ever.

After leaving Lorraine's place, he drove across town to Motel 6. Mentally, he wasn't ready to confront Curtis. He wanted to finish the beating he had previously begun. He didn't trust himself. Rage surged through him at Curtis.

Nevertheless, he was ready to do what God required of him.

Liam ground his teeth as he knocked on the motel room door. Within seconds, the door flew open.

"Son," Curtis' lips coiled into an evil smile.

That word coming from Curtis' mouth made Liam want to spit. Instead, he stood like a wall with shoulders squared, arms firmly at his side.

Curtis crossed his arms.

"I think you should know that in my quest for the truth," said Liam, "I uncovered some interesting facts. You've been busy since you arrived in Tallahassee. The authorities don't appreciate things like tampering with government documents or coercing government employees."

Liam fought the urge to punch Curtis until he pleaded for mercy. But vengeance did not belong to him.

"But I want you to know that I forgive you," said Liam.

Curtis tightened his jaw and shifted his weight. "What?"

"I forgive you."

"I didn't ask you to forgive me," said Curtis, with a slight catch in his voice. "I don't need your forgiveness."

"I forgive you for the lies, the schemes, and for whatever else you've done, intending to harm me, my brother, or someone that I love."

"I guess you think you know it all. Daisy …"

Liam silenced him with a controlled wave. "I forgive you, but I will not stand here and let you malign my mother. And if you come near me or my family again, I will turn you in to the authorities."

Liam turned and walked away. He entered his truck and drove away.

Chapter 31

Curtis stepped into the room and closed the door. He paced the floor. "You forgive me? What makes you think I want you to forgive me? You're gonna be a martyr now? You gonna make the great sacrifice?"

He pounded an angry fist in the air and continued, "Guess what? I was relieved when they took away my parental rights. I was happy to be free from the responsibility of two growing boys. And I didn't think twice about how your mother would raise you. I didn't care. And when I found out she'd placed you for adoption, I still didn't care. Do you forgive me for that?"

Curtis' heart pounded in his chest as he reached for a cigarette. He hadn't expected Liam to use the F word. "I wish I had been man enough to be the father you and your brother needed, but I wasn't. I barely cared for myself. How could I take care of a wife and two children?"

Surprise, confusion, frustration, and pride battled for a central place in his heart. He took a deep breath, trying to subdue the tempest of emotions raging inside him.

"Liam caught me off guard. I didn't expect him to forgive me. Why would he even offer it? I don't understand. If they had given me the chance, I could have been the father they needed."

He stopped for a moment, his perspective on what he had done shifting.

"But I was the one who gave up the chance to be their father," Curtis finally admitted. "If I hadn't been selfish, maybe things would have turned out differently. It's time I stopped causing so much pain."

He sat on the edge of the bed. "I've created a mess. Now I need to clean it. What can I do? I can't change the past. I should just leave town. That way, Liam will have his wedding as planned. He and Donnie can continue their happy life without me. Our paths will never cross again. But Liam and Donnie will always look over their shoulders, wondering when I will show up again. What kind of life is that?"

As he sat alone in his room, Curtis contemplated what he should do next. He knew it wouldn't be easy, but it had to be done. It was the only way to release the envy and jealousy he felt toward Daisy.

Chapter 32

Curtis parked his vehicle across the street from the church. After adjusting the seat, he got comfortable at the controls and observed guests coming to the ceremony. He spotted two police cars near the entrance of the building. A few men dressed in black, possibly security, surveyed the area.

"I guess I can assume my presence is not welcome here," he muttered with sarcasm.

A suggestive grin crossed his face as he saw a woman adjusting her dress. Then Curtis' thoughts shifted to the looming confrontation. It wouldn't be easy. Liam, Donnie, nor Daisy would be happy to see him. But this was the only way to put an end to the pain and the lies.

Chapter 33

Liam stood at the front of the church, surrounded by pillar candles and delicate twinkle lights woven into bare winter branches. The transformation turned the otherwise understated sanctuary into a winter wonderland. Along the altar stood pedestal arrangements in matte gold vessels with cream florals and frosted greenery.

Dressed in a black satin peak-lapel tuxedo, he looked every bit the part of an anxious groom. Liam tugged at the black silk bow tie. Then, he ran his fingers over the crisp ivory pleated shirt. The entire ensemble was more comfortable when he tried it on the day before the event.

He shifted his weight from foot to foot in his high-shine patent leather oxfords. Then, he planted both feet firmly, willing himself to stand still.

Donnie stood next to him, wearing a big grin and a cream tuxedo. "If you pass out, I'll catch you. I'm gonna laugh, but I'll catch you first."

"Haha."

"You may be the groom, but I still look better than you," said Donnie, failing in his second attempt at humor.

Liam's eyes fell upon his mother, sitting in the front row. She looked beautiful in her champagne off-the-shoulder gown. Liam didn't know how he felt about the long split that exposed her legs, but he realized his mother would always dress stylishly. Their gazes connected, and he mouthed, "I love you." She placed a hand over her heart, and tears made their way down her cheeks.

Zeke, who was sitting next to her, wrapped his arm around her. Grateful, Liam gave an appreciative nod. Although he wished his father were there to witness his nuptials, he was grateful for Zeke's presence in his mother's life.

Liam's eyes scanned the closed sanctuary doors, still and unmoved like the calm before the storm. He scanned the groomsmen, all dressed in cream tuxedos, standing at attention, trying not to smile. Then he scanned the faces in the crowd. Some familiar, others blurred by nerves.

He spotted Brandon standing at the rear of the sanctuary in full uniform. Sweat gathered on his forehead. The weight of the moment pressed into his chest. He turned to his brother and whispered, "I hope Curtis doesn't show up."

Donnie placed a hand on Liam's shoulder and squeezed. "We got this, bro. Everything will be fine. You see Brandon standing guard. And there's security at all the doors. Every one of the six groomsmen is ready, willing, and able to take him down."

"I hope you're right."

"Look at me."

Liam looked Donnie in the eye.

"You love Lorraine, and Lorraine loves you. That's all this moment needs to be about. Let peace guard your heart, man."

"You're right. Thanks, bro." Liam released a deep breath and reminded himself of what the day was all about.

I'm about to marry the most beautiful woman in the world. I'm going to spend the rest of my life making her happy, and together, we will accomplish great things.

I will allow nothing and no one to stop me from enjoying every minute of this day. I choose to think of God's goodness to me.

***

Lorraine stood behind the two doors, more akin to gateways to everything she'd wished for. Caught between memory and miracle, she pressed a trembling hand to her heart, grounding herself in the steady rhythm beneath the lace.

Her fingers trembled as they reached for her father's powerful arm. He looked at her, eyes full of more than words could carry, and gave a single nod.

She touched the edge of her veil, smoothed the bodice of her gown, and exhaled, slow and shaky.

"Thank you, God, for second chances, for Liam and for this love I thought I'd lost."

The first majestic notes of "Here Comes the Bride" rose like a promise in the air. Almost instantly, the music faded under the sound of her own thoughts.

This is it.

Then, with one final inhale, she stilled the flutter in her chest.

The doors opened, and a sea of faces turned in her direction. Some were smiling, some were weeping, and others were watching. Then everything else faded but the aisle, the light, and Liam. There he stood, waiting, eyes locked on hers like she was the only thing in the room.

Liam's knees went weak when he saw her. She stepped through the door, a vision in ivory and grace. The candlelight danced off the beading on her dress, and her veil floated like a sigh. His love was so powerful that it caused his eyes to water.

When she reached him, and the song ended, he exhaled. Mesmerized by her beauty, Liam heard Pastor Johnson's voice in the background. Dr. Davis released Lorraine's hand and placed it in his. Peace and promise settled in his chest.

The words were familiar: to have and to hold … in sickness and in health … as long as you both shall live.

Liam's voice didn't hesitate. Lorraine didn't hurry.

Pastor Johnson nodded, satisfied. "Now let us seal these vows with light and prayer."

They shifted to the unity candle. Two flames becoming one, the soft glow flickering.

And then …

"Lorraine and Liam," Pastor Johnson said, eyes twinkling. "What God has joined, let no one separate. I now pronounce you husband and wife. Liam, you may kiss your bride."

The exit doors of the church flew open, spilling soft light into the air. Liam and Lorraine walked out for the first time as husband and wife. They paused at the landing, hand in hand, hearts still racing. From their vantage point, they saw the city covered in evening silhouettes. The sun dipped low enough to wrap everything in a warm, honeyed hue. Family and friends waited below, laughing and hugging. Someone started a slow clap. It turned into a cheer.

Liam leaned in. "Check this out. We did it."

Lorraine grinned. "We really did."

Standing there, elevated on the steps, they felt as if they were on the edge of a new beginning.

"Are you ready, Mrs. Whittington?" asked Liam.

Lorraine smiled and answered. "Yes, I am, Mr. Whittington."

The air was sprinkled with laughter and rice as the newlyweds made their way through the cheering crowd. Daisy, Donnie, Zeke, and the wedding party followed close behind. Liam clutched Lorraine's hand, his smile wide and unguarded until the limousine came into view.

That's when he saw Curtis standing near the limousine.

Chapter 34

Liam's entire body stiffened when he saw Curtis. Instinctively, he placed himself in front of Lorraine and squared his shoulders. Donnie and the other groomsmen caught sight of each other, exchanging sharp looks. Within seconds, they surged forward, ready to drag him down.

The celebration faded around them, but in the circle by the limousine, silence reigned.

"That's the man from Motel 6," muttered Lorraine, her eyes narrowing. "Is this Curtis?"

"Yes. It is," said Liam.

With his hands stuffed deep into his pockets, Curtis said, "You and your brother were stolen from me."

Liam turned to Brandon as he approached Curtis. "This man is not a guest. Please escort him off the premises."

Gasps waved throughout the crowd, and all eyes turned to Curtis, who placed his hand in the air.

"I'm not breaking the law," said Curtis, sporting a smug expression.

Daisy stepped forward. Zeke stood next to her, ready to pounce if needed. "Then why are you here, Curtis? Why today?"

"You and your husband stole my boys from me."

"Stole?" asked Liam, his tone harsh. "No, Curtis, you handed us over when you walked away from your responsibility. You chose the streets over your sons. Nobody robbed you. When you disappeared, God blessed us with parents who taught us integrity, faith, and love. And you don't get to rewrite history."

Curtis opened his mouth to speak, but then Donnie stepped closer. "We will not let you poison this day or diminish the parents who raised us to be the men that we are today. You lost your chance years ago."

"We choose to honor the family God gave us. The only real family we've ever known," said Liam.

Curtis' eyes darted to Daisy, lingering a bit.

Daisy raised an eyebrow but remained silent. A mixture of shock and sympathy covered her face.

Liam edged closer, his arm still angled protectively in front of Lorraine. "Walk away, right now."

The crowd broke into applause. And with the cheers still resounding, Liam opened the limousine door to a future that was finally his.

Chapter 35

"Well, driver, what are we waiting for? Let's get the newlyweds on the road," said Donnie.

Liam looked at Daisy. With an approval nod and a quick hand wave, she rushed him on his way.

He leaned into Lorraine, resting his forehead against hers. "Are you ready?"

A big smile swept across her face. "Yes, let's do this."

Liam playfully bowed toward his bride. She giggled and responded with a tiny curtsy. Liam helped her inside. Before entering, Liam leaned in halfway and stole a quick kiss. "I love you."

"I love you, too."

The crowd roared.

Liam blew his mother a kiss, threw a fist pump in the air to his brother, and waved to the crowd. He stepped inside the limousine and closed the door. Feeling a sense of peace, he sank into the leather seat next to his bride. The clear pane between them and the driver rose, turning the back seat into their private sanctuary.

Liam looked at Lorraine with quiet desperation. He'd waited a long time to find a wife, a woman he could love and trust. A rush of warmth spread through him as reality set in.

She whispered, "What if …"

Whatever Lorraine was about to say dissolved the instant his lips found hers. The kiss, unyielding and hungry, carried his hope of the future.

When he finally pulled away, they sat there wrapped in each other's embrace. A sense of peace filled the air.

He looked into her eyes. "This is it. The beginning of the promise of us."

The end.

For now.

Discussion Questions

1. What emotions did you feel as Liam and Lorraine prepared for their wedding? Which moment felt the most real or relatable to you?

2. How did their past experiences shape the way they handled conflict and communication?

3. "Love was supposed to be simple—until life got in the way." How does this statement apply to Liam and Lorraine's journey?

4. In what ways did family expectations influence the choices both characters made? Have you ever faced similar pressure?

5. How do forgiveness and trust intertwine in this story? Which character's growth in these areas stood out to you most?

6. Lorraine faces a life-changing opportunity that challenges her idea of "forever." What does the story suggest about balancing love and ambition?

7. How does faith influence the decisions Liam and Lorraine make? Did you notice any moments where they had to lean on God more than each other?

8. Both characters carry emotional scars from the past. How does healing show up differently for each of them?

9. If you could give Liam or Lorraine one piece of advice before the wedding, what would it be?

10. How did humor and grace help lighten the heavier moments in the story?

11. The story takes place during Christmas—a season of love, hope, and new beginnings. How does the timing enhance the overall message?

12. What role do family and community play in helping Liam and Lorraine rediscover what matters most?

13. Were there any supporting characters whose wisdom or actions left a lasting impression on you?

14. "Forever" can mean different things to different people. How did your understanding of the word shift after reading this book?

15. How did the couple's challenges test their faith in God—and in each other?

16. Have you ever had to choose between your dreams and someone you love? How did that experience shape you?

17. What does The Promise of Us teach about grace—the kind we give ourselves and the kind we extend to others?

18. How do Liam and Lorraine's struggles mirror real-life relationships? Which moment or conversation felt the most authentic?

19. The story closes with a sense of quiet redemption. What do you think that means for their future together?

20. If this book had a theme song, what would it be—and why?

About the Author

W. Mason Dunn is a best-selling author who is passionate about spreading the Gospel through her literary works. She has written and published seven novels with many more in development.

Born in Bossier City, Louisiana, W. Mason Dunn values continuous learning and self-improvement. She earned an undergraduate degree in Business Administration from Texas College and a graduate degree in Public Administration from the University of Oklahoma.

With over two decades of experience as a higher education counselor for the military, she gained invaluable insights while traveling extensively with her husband during his 20 years of distinguished service in the United States Marine Corps. These personal and professional experiences have deeply influenced her storytelling.

W. Mason Dunn is a devoted wife of nearly four decades to her husband, Donald, and the proud mother of two adult children, Ashley and Michael Dunn. When she is not working on her next literary project, she enjoys reading, playing Scrabble, solving crossword puzzles, and helping others.

Other Books by W Mason Dunn

Great stories are even better when they're shared. If *The Promise of Us* touched you, here are a few simple ways to help it find its next reader:

1. Leave a review on Amazon. It only takes a minute, but it makes a world of difference.

2. Snap a pic and share it on social media. Tell folks what you loved most—whether it was a character, a moment, or just the way it made you feel.

3. Pass it on. Send a note to a friend who'd enjoy it too—or better yet, surprise them with a copy.

Thanks so much for reading. I'm so glad you spent time with this story.